The Blonde Murders:
A Detective Sara Nichols Mystery

G. WAYNE TILMAN

WOLFPACK
PUBLISHING
— EST 2013 —

Published in the United States by Wolfpack Publishing, Las Vegas

Wolfpack Publishing
6032 Wheat Penny Avenue
Las Vegas, NV 89122

wolfpackpublishing.com

Paperback ISBN 978-1-64734-893-9
eBook ISBN 978-1-64734-892-2

The Blonde Murders:
A Detective Sara Nichols Mystery

PROLOGUE
TEN YEARS AGO

Rose Douglas was propped up in her bed, wearing a negligee that barely hid her perfect body. She was beautiful, successful, and both good and very bad. Rose ran what she liked to call the "best little whorehouse in Georgia." Like its fictional Texas twin, a slightly corrupt sheriff who was her brother-in-law and devoted friend, greatly facilitated her operation.

What had started as a conversation was rapidly deteriorating into an argument. It was not hot and loud; rather, it was quiet and deadly cold. Rose glanced at the pearl-handled straight razor sitting on the bedside table. It was the last thing she did on this earth. A strong hand clasped over her face and another picked up the razor and Rose Douglas died with a crimson gurgle. A quick search of the room yielded a lockbox, later to be found containing a large amount of cash and a diary. The former was seed money for the things to follow; the diary was the guide.

CHAPTER 1
PRESENT DAY

Mary Ann Hixon was red-haired, green-eyed and a catch. She was five foot-eight with a voluptuous body on the "pleasingly plump" side of "a bit overweight." That body was accentuated by a skintight emerald sheath that did not even pretend to hide the fact that she wore nothing underneath it. The red 3" heels were gorgeous and were good Christian Louboutin knock-offs. It was Friday night and she was driving to Ft. Myers for fun and games at a club she particularly liked. She had worked all week at a clothing store at an Osprey County mall on US 41 and had had enough of customers who insisted they could get into size ten dresses, when a sixteen would be tight. She did not even begin to think that, in a couple of years, she would be them. "Give it up, bitches" she thought.

She held the red Corolla to the speed limit, having had a line of coke before leaving her marina apartment. No need to have to deal with the Florida Highway Patrol or a local deputy and mess up a potentially great night. If she got really lucky—a potentially great weekend.

Mary Ann made it to the club without incident and parked the compact. She went in and slipped immediately into the restroom for a quick review of war paint. She decided that neither she, a Hollywood makeup artist, nor probably even God, could improve upon the reflection in the mirror, so she made her entrance.

The club's guests gave her the response she wanted, they were agape at her stunning face, hair and body. But, these guests were not what she wanted, though the evening was very young yet. The group sitting alone, two by two, or at tables for four, were older and not that attractive. She even spotted a couple of Mullet hairdos in the crowd. "No, no. Not a good sign."

She ordered a Jack and Coke, now called a "Lemmy" in honor of the late Motorhead front man whose favorite it was. She still called it by its ingredient name and probably always would.

A girl band was playing. They were rockers with not much in the way of clothes and lots in the way of body art. Mary Ann, who did not have any tattoos or piercings, studied them. What the hell else did she have to do until a more interesting crowd made its appearance?

The lead guitarist was cute, in a raven-haired, pierced, Goth sort of way. Her voice was Julie London smoky, but probably from too many cigarettes, another turn-off. So, Mary Ann downed her drink and motioned for another.

By the third Jack and Coke, Mary Ann was a little less particular about the crowd. She perked up as a new arrival walked in and up to the bar to order a drink.

The new arrival was probably two or three inches taller than Mary Ann, with similar-sized heels. Her legs were long, breasts were hidden by a wrap, but seemed to push the wrap out nicely. Her hair was blonde and long.

She turned with a wine glass and looked for a place to sit. Mary Ann had been there an hour and the club was filling fast. The woman looked at her and smiled. Thinking this was the second most attractive person there, behind her, Mary Ann smiled back and motioned her over.

"Hi. You are a lifesaver." The voice had a husky sexiness, not unlike the singer on stage would croon in some rock ballad.

"Have a seat. It almost looks like us against them," Mary Ann said referring to the older lesbians in the club.

"Yep, dyke night. Except for you. I am Allie."

"Hi, Allie. I am Mary Ann."

"What do you do when you are not dazzling people in this club?" Allie asked.

Mary Ann smiled at that. "Charm is always nice," she thought.

"Oh, I work in retail a bit south of here."

"Must be high fashion, based on your outfit!"

"Well, it is fashion, but not quite the runway in New York or Paris."

Allie smiled, perfect white teeth showing. "Or, I guess Miami, huh?"

"Yes, certainly Miami is a fashion center now. What do you do?"

"What I do is really exciting. I hesitate to tell you, it's so exciting."

"Oh, come on. Tell me!"

"I'm a CPA."

"Well, it may not be that exciting, but it probably is lucrative."

"I do okay. Luckily, I have enough corporate customers that it is not as seasonal as it could be. But, there are months where I choose to play more than work. I could work and make more money, but, why?"

"Why, indeed! I like the way you look at life. I wish I could afford to do that!"

"Mary Ann, what do you like to do?"

"Oh, fun stuff. Explore new restaurants. I have a paddle board, so I paddle the Greenway," she said referring to the long local canoe and kayak trail along the coast.

"Girlfriends? Boyfriends?"

"Why would I be here if I had a boyfriend?"

"You could be a housewife out following up on an experimentation in college. You could be bi. Lots of personal reasons. You could be a journalist doing research."

"None of those. I am a non-advertised—this is Hicksville you know—card-carrying lesbian. I like tacos, not wieners. Now, how about you?"

"I am firmly in your camp! Maybe, if the night progresses like I hope it will, I will prove how firmly to you."

"Is that a dare?"

"More like a fond wish."

"Hmm."

They talked more and drank more. Mary Ann had barely enough coke left for two lines, but shared it with Allie in the restroom.

By midnight, they were ready to leave. To where was undetermined. Finally, they agreed that Allie would follow Mary Ann back to her apartment.

******

At the apartment complex twenty minutes later, Allie pulled off to the side and parked at the gate. She got in with Mary Ann, using the tissue in her hand to avoid leaving fingerprints on the door handles or seat belt latches. There was a pedestrian exit gate that did not require a code to leave. Allie convinced Mary Ann that would be simpler in the morning. Or, if they chose to get breakfast out, she would ride with Mary Ann to pick up her car.

Entering the one-bedroom apartment in a complex that cost Mary Ann more than she should have been budgeting for lodging, Allie said "Point me to whatever alcohol you have. I will make drinks while you get comfortable. I am hoping very comfortable."

"How do you define 'very?'"

"I cannot wait to see, touch and kiss every inch of what I think is going to be an absolutely perfect body!"

"I can arrange that. The booze is in the lower cabinet beside the sink in the kitchen. The glasses are in the right top cabinet and the mixers are in the refrigerator. I will be in the bedroom, getting 'very.'"

She walked off, beginning to undress just to tease and tempt her guest, all the time wishing she had spent a little more time at the apartment's gym instead of sitting at its pool.

Allie went into the kitchen, but touched nothing. She slipped her dress off, stepped out of her panties and shoes and stood stark naked in the center of the kitchen,

In two minutes, Mary Ann walked out. She still had the red-soled knock-offs on, but nothing else. She was stunning. A perfect 38D without enhancement, a little curve to the belly, and beautiful legs to match.

Allie held out her arms and Mary Ann flew into them. After a long, deep kiss, Allie playfully tugged Mary Lee's red locks back, exposing her throat. She kissed the neck and Mary Ann moaned. She began to massage Mary Ann's breasts, then dropped her hand lower. And, lower.

As Mary Ann was getting into the touches, Allie reached up and took Mary Ann's head in both hands and twisted it roughly to the left. Before Mary Ann could protest, Allie reached to the counter and picked up a straight razor she had placed there and slid it across Mary Ann's neck, the crimson spraying away from Allie and onto the counter, wall and floor.

Eyes locked open in horror, Mary Ann collapsed to the puddle in the floor and added to its rapid increase.

Allie said, "Damn bitch. I could have been you, but no," picked up a dish cloth and proceeded to wipe anything she may have touched entering the apartment. Inspecting herself, she found that her care had worked. No blood spatter on her. She quickly re-dressed. Looking carefully before exiting the door, she walked at a normal pace to the pedestrian gate and went through it, the dish cloth covering her hand to avoid leaving telltale fingerprints. She was sure that she had left none. She also knew that apartment complexes this expensive should have had surveillance security cameras. That it did not was the first thing she had noticed upon entering and that absence had greatly facilitated her plan.

Allie unlocked, got into her dark gray Altima, and left. No one had seen her come. No one had seen her go. Except for one beautiful dead girl. Life was good. This was an ideal date, Allie thought.

******

By ten o'clock the next morning, sixty-year old Brenda Kilgallen, owner of Brenda's Frocks, was worried. Mary Ann had not been late for work in the two years she had worked at Brenda's. Now, she was an hour and a half late. Brenda had called Mary Ann's cell phone repeatedly, but with no luck reaching her friend and employee. It was a small shop and there was only one other employee, a young black woman named Sophia. Brenda had called Sophia and asked her to come in early to cover and Sophia had agreed.

"I just don't know what's going on, this is just not like Mary Ann," she commented to her other employee.

"Hey, Friday is date night. Maybe she got lucky," Sophia had responded.

"You mean she could be shacked up with some man and ignoring my calls?"

Sophia turned away so her naïve boss would not see her roll her big brown eyes, "Yeah, something like that. Or, what worries me more, maybe she's sick—ate something that gave her an allergic attack. Or, fell down. We should send somebody to check on her. Or, go ourselves."

"We can't go. It's Saturday, our best day and the shop is open. Should we call the fire department?"

"We should call somebody. Why don't you get her address out of your files? They will need that, because we don't know what it is."

"Good idea. Then, I will call 911 and they will send the fire department!"

Brenda pulled open a desk drawer, fingered through some files and pulled the one that said "Mary Ann Hixon" on the tab. She pulled out the application and saw that the address had been struck through and a new one written in. She noted that on a post-it note, along with Mary Ann's cell phone number. She knew that Mary Ann did not have a regular house phone.

She took a deep breath and dialed 911.

"Osprey County 911. What is your emergency?"

"I don't know if this is an emergency. I have an employee who is hours late for work and that's just not like her. I am afraid she might be sick or something. Can you send the fire department by to check on her?"

"Ma'am, what's her address?"

"The Sunview Apartments, 719 Sunview Circle, apartment number B."

The dispatcher paused for a moment, then came back on the line.

"Okay, that's unincorporated county, so I will send an Osprey deputy. What is the person's name?"

"Mary Ann Hixon."

"How about her age and description?"

"She's white, late twenties, light strawberry blonde hair. Real pretty. Good figure, but runs to the voluptuous, if you know what I mean. Tall enough to pull it off."

"Does she have any medical problems that are known to you? Seizures? Heart? Diabetic?"

"Oh, no. Nothing like that that I know of. Sophia? Does Mary Ann have any medical issues?" Receiving a negative nod form Sophia, Brenda confirmed, "No, we don't think so."

"Okay, Ma'am. I will have a deputy do a wellness check. I have captured your number. Is this a good one to call back on when we have something to report?"

"Yes, it is, officer. Thank you so much."

Brenda hung up. Sophia had walked into the office when Brenda had called out to her about the medical history. "Okay, I've done it. They are going to send a deputy and let us know. I hope everything is okay and she just overslept."

"I hope so, too," Sophia responded, though she considered that possibility far more unlikely than the owner did.

******

"Unit 2017, respond to Sunview Apartments, 719 Sunview Circle, number B on a wellness check. Subject is white female, twenties, blonde hair, medium to heavy build, no known medical issues."

"Radio, 2017. Mark me en route, with an ETA of twelve or fifteen minutes."

"Copy."

Thirteen minutes later, Deputy Shane Hilliard went through the apartment gate, using the first responder password, and found Sunview Circle. He located the 719 building and parked his Tahoe. The deputy went up to the steps and knocked on the door hard enough to wake anyone asleep inside. There was no response. He walked around the building and counted apartments until he located the correct patio. The gate and fence were only waist high, so he stepped over. He looked in the sliding patio door to the kitchen and saw the subject of his check laying on the floor in a pool of blood. He could see that rigor mortis had already set in, so there was no need to break in the door and try to render first aid.

Deputy Hilliard quickly walked around the building to his SUV and keyed the radio mic. The radio system was encrypted, so he knew his transmission would be unavailable to people with scanners.

"2017 Rush!"

"Go, 2017."

"Subject located. I'm gonna need a supervisor, crime scene unit, detective, and ME."

"No question about the victim status? And, does it appear to be natural causes or homicide? Could perp still be there, if homicide?"

"No question, Radio. It's either homicide or suicide. Rigor mortis has set in, so I doubt the attacker, if there was one, is still inside. This one happened hours ago, I believe."

"Copy. Stand by. Units 3018, 4029, and CSI-1 respond to 719 Sunview Circle to meet 2017 on a DOA by violent means."

"Radio, this is 4029."

"Go ahead, Detective."

"I am on the other side of the county. Have 2017 and the sergeant, 3018, secure the scene until I get there. Ditto CSI-1, copy?"

"Units copy?"

All did.

The five foot eleven, fit detective with dark brown hair and sky-blue eyes knew the distance to be covered was almost thirty miles. It was not a lights and siren call; the victim was dead, for God's sake. But, it was important to view the scene and think about it before the world got involved. So, the detective pushed the accelerator on the hemi-powered unmarked Charger to the floor upon pulling onto US-41, the Tamiami Trail. Lights might be used if necessary, but most people, even tourists, recognized the dark gray charger with big black tires and several antennae for what it was...a cop car, and one in a big hurry.

Detective Nichols drove fast and smoothly. The three hundred seventy horsepower V8 roared when pushed, and the car virtually flew past slower vehicles. When traffic became heavier, the LED wig-wag or alternately flashing headlights and the blue windshield lights warned drivers over, along with a blip on the siren or air horn.

Twenty minutes later, the gray sedan pulled into the apartment complex. Locating the address was greatly simplified by the police vehicles and the Medical Examiner's van parked at various angles outside of the painted parking spots.

The detective spotted the ME's issue sedan parked and grinned. The county medical examiner, Dr. Lynn Goddard was one hot proposition. She looked more like a movie star than a doctor who did autopsies and helped solve crimes. And, Detective Nichols frequently enjoyed nights and mornings...and sometimes afternoons, with the good doctor. This was a friendship that no one else in the county knew about.

Hearing, then viewing the detective's arrival, the crusty sergeant walked out, his cowboy boots as appropriate to the West Coast of Florida as they would have been to Texas.

"Hiya, Sara! This looks like a messy one. We got the door open, and checked the apartment for more victims, retrieved her purse from the bedroom for identification, but did not go in the kitchen where the late Ms. Hixon is located. There did not seem to be any blood elsewhere in the apartment, so I'm thinking the murder occurred where she fell."

"Joe, if that's your take, it will probably be mine, too. Let's go look at her. How long has Dr. Goddard been here?"

"Maybe four or five minutes before you roared in. I gotta tell you, Sara. You sure can drive that car!"

She gave him her Wonder Woman smile. "God, girl. That even lights up Florida sunshiny days."

"Hey, Joe. When ya got it, ya got it!"

They walked into the apartment. She saw Dr. Goddard kneeling on a plastic sheet she had put on the puddle of blood to access the body.

The victim was naked and appeared to have been quite beautiful.

"Hey, Lynn."

"Wondered when you'd get here. Where have you been?"

"I responded from almost thirty miles away."

"Made good time."

"Argo moves when I spur him."

"You and that damn car. One of these days they are going to give you an official subcompact with twelve horsepower. Who again was 'Argo?'"

"Then, I'll find a new agency. Argo was Warrior Princess Xena's palomino charger. Now, he's mine. Don't go there. What's the TOD?"

"I just checked that. Looks like time of death is around midnight. At least that's what is going on the death certificate."

"Death by?"

"Head apparently jerked to side to avoid the spray, when he slit her throat with something really sharp. Can't say until the autopsy, but my guess is a razor or darn sharp knife."

"Had a chance to look for rape or sex? I could really use some DNA markers for when I get this asshole."

"Cursory look says 'no.' Again, more Monday morning at the autopsy. Be there or be square."

"I will. Joe thinks she was killed right here. You buy into that, too?"

"Probably. I have not done your job and investigated the whole apartment, but everything seems clean. Looks like she was killed here, and bled out here. Pretty girl. A real tragedy."

"Yep. But, all murders are tragedies one way or the other."

Dr. Lynn Goddard responded "Everybody is somebody's kid. Somebody, somewhere, is probably going to be suffering."

"Maybe."

"Lynn," Sara began," if you want to bag and remove her, we will start the forensic investigation. And, I will see you at your regular 0900 time Monday for the autopsy."

The two exchanged bland glances that said, "I'll call you tonight," but no one else in the kitchen noticed, experienced peace officers or not.

Three hours later, Sara taped up the apartment as a crime scene and had a workman put a different lock on the door. The key was one only used by the Osprey County Sheriff's Office and would keep the apartment manager and maintenance and anyone else but her out. She, the sergeant, Deputy Hubbard and one other deputy had interviewed virtually everyone in the apartment complex with no joy.

The only two bits of new information were her place of employment from a neighbor and her next of kin from the resident manager, who had been summoned once it had been determined that a murder had occurred on her property. Sara had dispatch contact Jacksonville Sheriff's Office to make the notification to Mary Ann Hixon's parents. Since the City of Jacksonville and Duval County merged some years ago, the Sheriff's Office and police department had merged.

Sara thought about the lack of other useful information from the neighbors.

It was not like this place was Ft. Apache the Bronx, where nobody ever saw anything. It was a bad design. Sara had learned about CPTED in a continuing education course. Crime Prevention Through Environmental Design would have helped here. In the past, people had sat on their front porches and waved at passersby.

Now, too many houses and apartments, Sara thought, were designed where all the living space was in the rear, and nobody could see what was going on in their neighborhoods. It was a damn shame. And, a direct contradiction to what CPTED suggested.

During the forensic investigation, she had added several things to her case notes, none of which would lead to the apprehension of the murderer. She had learned from the blood spray analysis that Mary Ann had died where she fell. A thorough fingerprint dusting of the apartment had not given any prints but the tenant's. Nothing requiring elimination prints at all. She had learned that there was no tampering of the windows or doors, so a break-in was not likely. Ms. Hixon had apparently let the person in and undressed for them. She was also, unless something new came out of the autopsy, killed prior to sex.

Nothing was broken or disturbed suggesting no fight had occurred. Her purse still had money and credit cards in it, so robbery did not appear to be a motive. There were no defensive marks on her body; her nails with the square French manicure did not have bits of DNA underneath from scratching at her attacker.

It looked like a cold-blooded murder by dictionary definition.

Dusting of the victim's car had not yielded any prints inside or out except for hers, so if the attacker had ridden in it, he had worn gloves.

After closing the crime scene, Sara had an idea. She walked to the front of the complex and used her small field kit to dust the handle on the pedestrian exit gate for latent prints. Using her tactical flashlight, since it was getting dark, she could see smudges on the round handle, but nothing definable as fingerprints. She felt that the person exiting, murderer or otherwise, had deliberately smudged the knob to destroy any evidentiary prints.

Sara got the sick feeling in the pit of her stomach that she usually got when she knew she was up against someone who was careful and smart. Solving gang and drug murders was easier. A little money, a lot of threats and somebody talked. This was not going to be that easy.

She got in Argo and drove to the Sheriff's complex and went into her cubicle. Sara wrote a detailed initial report in the format she had learned while a special agent for the Navy's Criminal Investigative Service. She put it in the lieutenant's in-box. He was old school and liked to hold paper instead of reading a screen. The Sheriff's Office was small enough that the Investigative Division was headed by a lieutenant, had three detectives, including Sara, a pair of two-person CSI units and, soon, a crime analyst.

The CSI team had picked up the victim's cell phone and laptop computer to see if they had anything of value, like a selfie with a murderer. Stranger things had happened. Many gang bangers where shocked when their personal videos of themselves shooting up a house, then waving their guns around while bragging about it, showed up in court as proof of their guilt.

Sara drove home, arriving at her three-bedroom typical Florida stucco ranch by eight at night. She hit the garage opener on the Charger's driver side sun visor and parked next to her Jeep Wrangler two-door hardtop. She sat there for a minute. How lucky could a girl be? A hemi with a gas card and a siren for work, and an orange Jeep she called "Tangelo" for play. It did not get any better than that, she thought.

She unlocked the door between the garage and the utility room and rushed to disarm her alarm system. Her Sphynx cats Gibbs and DiNozzo, met her as she moved quickly to the alarm panel. They almost tripped her, doing circle eights around her ankles as she spoke with them lovingly and keyed the disarm code.

She generally dressed in an Osprey Sheriff golf shirt, khakis, running shoes and wore her gun, gold star, handcuffs and magazine holder in plain sight. Sara kicked off her shoes and slipped the Sig automatic out of the holster. Thus unencumbered, she sat on the sofa as both hairless cats jumped into her lap and crawled up her chest.

Once she had proven to the felines that they were all that mattered in the entire world, she walked into the bedroom and stripped.

She looked at herself in the mirror. She had started college at her father's alma mater, Virginia Tech, but had gotten a beach volleyball full-ride scholarship at the University of Miami and had used the scholarship for the first degree in her Criminal Justice baccalaureate and master's degrees. Sara had played pro beach volleyball for two years before going into law enforcement. She still had the long, lithe body, but her cup size had increased rather pleasingly, she thought, along the way. She turned and posed, blew a kiss to herself and walked into the kitchen. She got out a Heinie and opened it as she walked out to the solar-heated pool. She eased into the water and onto a raft. After sipping the beer, she placed it into the holder built into the raft and just floated, looking through the pool cage screen at the stars that had finally come out.

After totally mellowing out, she put on a tee shirt, decided to skip dinner, and called Lynn.

"Hey, Foxy Doc. Whatcha doing?"

"Getting ready to go to bed. You?"

"Same. Want to do some stand up paddle boarding tomorrow?"

"Let's take kayaks instead, so we can take food and drink easier. I think I'd rather exercise on my ass anyway."

"That makes two of us."

"You'd rather exercise on your ass?"

"Nope. Yours."

"Sex fiend with a gun."

"Ha! Sex fiend with a little black bag...you do have a doctor's bag don't you?"

"Hell no! You think I make house calls or something?"

"You made a house call to my house."

"That's right! You had a black eye, beat up knuckles and a contusion on your shin where some perp kicked the crap out of you."

"Might I remind you that he was taken to the hospital in the cuffs I put on him?"

"Oh, yeah. Xena, Warrior Princess."

"Don't you forget that, okay?"

"I won't, Sweetie! You know I consider you my personal superhero."

"I know. Because I am. I'll see you in the morning and we can work out paddling details, okay?"

"Okay. Nighty!"

Sara disconnected. She got up, armed her alarm system and put the 9mm pistol by her bed. Two hairless "naked" cats jumped up and she turned off the light. Prayers and a lot of purring, and she was asleep in no time.

The next morning, she put a K-cup in the Keurig and brewed the first of probably six cups of black coffee for the day. She called Lynn and set the kayak trip for eleven. She had to check on several tenants who were not at home during yesterday's apartment canvas first.

After two hours of waking apartment dwellers up and finding out nothing, Sara stopped at the park where she and Lynn planned to meet and changed in the ladies' room. She had a padlock-secured steel box in her Jeep and put her gun, badge and other gear into that, along with the official golf shirt. She kept her laminated Sheriff's ID card in the wet box along with a small, but very powerful backup revolver. She was, after all, an Osprey detective 24/7.

Wearing a bikini and a tee shirt from a mudder endurance run, she lifted the fourteen-foot kayak down from the Jeep she had driven to the apartments. It simply was not worth driving her official car, then having to go fifteen miles' home...

By the time Sara had gotten the sea kayak, her paddle and dry bag and a cooler bag with slices of fruit, cheeses, crackers and bottles of water at the launch, she saw Lynn's small BMW SUV pull in. She helped her friend unload a similar cargo and the two paddled off to explore a small portion of the hundred ninety-mile Calusa Blueway canoe and kayak trail.

They paddled for an hour and spotted a stretch of beach suitable for a picnic. Beaching the two kayaks, they set out the food and drinks on a beach towel and swam briefly. The Blueway was fairly crowded on a Sunday and both were public officials and recognizable, so they portrayed themselves as they were—two good friends—and left anything else for later. Lynn lamented the opportunity to skinny dip, one of her favorite things.

On the way back, they were paddling against a strong tide; luckily both women had kayaks with rudders and were able to maintain relatively straight paths back to the launch point. They carried the kayaks back to their vehicles and placed them on the roof racks.

While securing the roof racks and chatting about which house they would go to for dinner, or whether to choose a waterfront bistro with atmosphere and too much fried seafood, a loud argument broke out at a large family gathering at the park pavilion near where they had moved their vehicles to re-pack them.

As Lynn continued talking about dinner, Sara's attention was increasingly drawn to the argument.

A short, strong man with a potbelly and an appropriate wife-beater shirt was berating a woman who was, presumptively, his wife. Other family members, both male and female were attempting to separate the two, but he broke loose and took a swing at the woman. It connected and she fell back against a wooden picnic table.

Sara opened the steel chest in the Jeep and stuck her gun and a pair of handcuffs in the back of her bikini bottom, hidden by the tee. She dropped the lanyard holding the Sheriff's ID around her neck. By this time, her friend the ME, had processed what was going on and was getting her phone out.

"Lynn, call now and get somebody rolling, but stay on the line to speed them up if it gets ugly, so you can tell them I need assistance. The trouble with these things is you help one and the rest—including the victim—turn on you," she spoke in low tones to her friend.

Sara walked over to the pavilion as the man reached out and dragged the woman to her feet.

"Sheriff's Office! Step away from the woman, and I mean now!"

The man shoved the woman back down and turned to her, trying to focus more clearly thought his beer vision.

He stood, legs apart and got a large grin on his face, a bit of spittle running down the left side of his mouth. The family members stepped back, all were surprised and some were even sober enough to realize that the situation had just escalated beyond a point where their abusive relative could come out well.

"Show me a badge, bitch!"

Sara held the ID strung around her neck and said, "Try to focus on this, if you can. It says I am a detective with the Osprey County Sheriff's Office. Just so you will know, I watched you hit that woman. She does not have to prefer charges under Florida law. But, I do. You are under arrest for domestic battery. Now, turn around and put your hands behind you."

"Any bitch that big has to be a dyke!"

"Sir, turn around now."

She watched as he tried to process the best action to take and realized he was going to take the worst one. Sara move her left leg out and back and assumed a defensive posture as he rushed her. He lowered his head to butt her. Sara stepped to the side and grabbed his neck and pushed down with her left hand, while tripping him with her left leg. He went down with an "Oof!"

Apparently an experienced fighter, even though he went down hard, he came back up quickly and spun around on her, charging again. She did a front snap kick into his groin and a knife edge blow to the back of his neck as he doubled over. This time, he did not immediately rise and she took the opportunity to drop on his back, her knee diagonally across it. She took one hand and moved it behind him. As he began to struggle, she applied a pressure hold and he screamed out. Several of the males in the group moved forward as she put the handcuff on his left wrist. She held her right hand out, palm towards them and said, "Back. Do not interfere or you will be arrested, too!"

Three moved forward and two things happened simultaneously. Sara reached behind her and drew the gun, pointing it at the three. And, Lynn, already identified to 911 as the county ME, spoke four words: "Officer needs assistance, now!"

The three began to back away. A county deputy was nearby and got the call. The siren was immediately heard by the people in the park, and a white Ford SUV with green markings and red and blue lights sped into the park within minutes. It was Deputy Shane Hilliard.

He stepped out of the vehicle, his own gun drawn and covering the three.

"Get on the ground! Do it now!" he growled.

As the men complied, he cuffed one. He knew another two or three cars would be arriving shortly and waited, his knee, like Sara's, on his prisoner and gun on the other two.

They stayed like this for a long several minutes, hearing the responding units before seeing them. Dr. Goddard motioned the woman who had been struck over to her car and quickly examined her. She had a dislocated jaw and was missing one tooth. The ME called 911 back and asked for them to respond a fire/rescue unit to check the woman.

The next unit to arrive was a sergeant, who assessed the situation and slowed other responding deputies. He handcuffed the other two and then the original attacker and his three family members were searched. They moved the prisoners behind the police cars away from both family members and park onlookers. Upon finding that the three did not actually threaten the detective, he read them the riot act, ran them for records and took their information.

"I have the right to arrest all three of you for interfering with an officer in the rightful performance of her duties. That means carrying your butts to the jail, getting you printed and photographed, having a nice body cavity search, and putting you in orange jump suits. I bet that would make your families here proud. Not to mention the pride your bosses would feel when you don't bond out in time for work tomorrow.

"Now, I'm willing to meet you halfway. You look at me in any way I consider unfriendly or disrespectful and the cuffs stay on and the ride to the jail goes as planned. You agree that what you were going to do was stupid and you will never be that stupid again, and I will uncuff you and you can go home without embarrassing your families here any further. What do you want to do? One at a time."

All took the deal. The attacker was not so lucky. He was

charged and went to the jail in Deputy Hubbard's unit. Sara would stop by and fill out the charge sheet during the man's jail processing. The victim's dislocation was sufficient that the paramedics took her to the regional medical center. The second deputy to arrive followed and made sure that a county domestic abuse counselor was assigned.

Before the law enforcement units left for the jail, hospital or to resume patrol, Sara thanked each for coming to help her.

The sergeant, a forty-five-year-old former Marine named Syl Jones, said "Sara, it looked to me like you had the situation well in hand before we got here."

"Not really, Syl. I couldn't let three jump me and all four disarm me, so I would have had to shoot somebody. Maybe everybody. Righteous or not, what a mess that would have been."

The sergeant and the two deputies grinned at her. She had knocked the living daylights out of the wife abuser and they suspected that she could have taken on the other three without having to fire a shot. But, the call for assistance was justified and they were glad to have been close enough to keep things from escalating further.

"It's always exciting being around you," Lynn started after the responders had left and they finished packing their vehicles.

"Don't start on me. You know good and damn well that you would not have let that bozo beat the woman. Right?"

"Right. But, I don't have handcuffs and I am much too pretty to chance fighting, so I would have just shot the bastard."

"Do you even have a gun with you?"

"I have my .38 snub nose and some pepper spray. A detective once told me to have a non-lethal alternative along with my gun. I almost always listen to her."

"As well you should. She's almost always right. And, now she has to go to the jail and sign the arrest papers for mister he-man. When he was face down with me on his back pinning him, I wanted so badly to whisper in his ear 'if I am a dyke because I am big or tall, then that must mean you are gay because you are short and sissy looking.'"

"That would have been priceless! Of course, you would probably have been sued or something."

"Yeah, or something."

"Since you have the paperwork to sign, let's eat at my place. I will go and fix something. You probably ought to put pants on before going to the jail. You can wash the park dirt off your knees and elbows at my house before getting into the spa."

"You're on! I will see you in less than an hour, I hope."

"Good! I have some fresh grouper filets and a new white wine for us to test."

CHAPTER 2

The grouper fillet was done en Papillote and had lemons, limes, sweet onions, wine, and Rose peppers inside the paper for flavoring. Lynn had fixed a simple green salad and prepared rice as a side dish. The experimental white wine was a disappointment, but too expensive to pour down the drain, so they drank it anyway.

Lynn lived in a harbor side townhouse with a community pool. For more personal use, she had a spa behind the patio privacy fence on the ground level. It was to that location the two retreated after dinner to finish the almost okay wine.

"Okay, Sara. We could not do it today because of being recognized, but I am going to do it now," Lynn said, slipping off her sundress, sandals and panties and stepping into the bubbling spa seductively.

The detective looked at her, a pleasant smile that signaled nothing—neither approval, nor disapproval.

"What? What kind of look is that? You should have an expression of abject awe!"

"Gotcha with my poker face! Sucka!"

Sara, with quick moves, disrobed and slipped into the spa. She sat across from her friend, looking now like the cat that just finished the milk and the fish.

An hour later, the large bottle of wine was gone and

the two lovely women were beginning to do their prune imitations. They got out somewhat shakily, wrapped in large towels, and went into the kitchen.

"You have had too much wine to drive home, ya know?"

"I have to go back and check on the boys. Plus, I have a long day tomorrow, starting with you and the autopsy, the first hearing on 'bozo the wife punching hero', interviews with the people where the victim worked, and looking into my other twelve open cases."

"In that case, I'd better make coffee and a lot of it!"

"Good idea. Will your hands be steady enough tomorrow for the autopsy?"

"Why? You think I'll slip and accidentally kill her?"

"Good point."

Three cups of black coffee later, and a lot of walking around, and Sara bid the beautiful ME goodnight and very carefully drove the Jeep home. She had to off-load the kayak before pulling into her garage. Those steps accomplished, she went into the house, greeted her two young men amid lots of purring on their part, dropped her clothes in a pile on the floor and collapsed on the bed. She knew her smart phone weekday alarm would awaken her at six in the morning, the house burglar alarm was set, the cats were fine, and to hell with about everything else until six.

Sara's eyes were still closed, but she felt she was being stared at. Neither cat was pressed against her. If someone had by-passed the alarm (she had set it last night, hadn't she?), neither were actually trained attack cats. Trained scaredy cats was more like it. She could roll left and retrieve her 9mm off the bedside table, assuming she put it in its usual place last night. She really was going to have to stop drinking. Or, maybe this was the guy with the razor and her resolutions would not matter.

"Oh, shit," she thought. "Enough is enough. I am going

to have to open my eyes and meet this head on." So, she did and saw Gibbs sitting on the bed next to her staring intently at her. On the other side, his brother, DiNozzo, was doing exactly the same thing.

"Wow. You'd think I could tell the difference between a hungry cat stare and a crazed razor-killer by now, huh?" The cats said nothing, but did continue staring until she got up and fed them. Thirty minutes, two cups of coffee and a shower later, the phone alarm went off signaling time to get up.

Today, Sara wore tan cargo pants instead of more formal slacks. She had to admit, wearing one of the many iterations of her Osprey Sheriff polo shirts daily with slacks simplified wardrobe expense, selection and cleaning. She really hated ironing and would go to illogical extremes to avoid it. She gave more than a passing thought to moving to Pasco County, nudist capital of the US, when she retired and avoid the whole wardrobe issue. She could get a mobile home in a resort and buy a golf cart. Not. Naked did not bother her. But, what in hell kind of heroic name could she give a golf cart?

Thanks to Gibbs and DiNozzo, she was out and about an hour early, so she went to the Osprey Café and one of the delightful old "gals," as they called themselves, took her order for a feta and spinach omelet with wheat toast and grits. She never understood why people from the North (which she defined as anywhere north or west of the Mason-Dixon Line, since south was the South and east was the Atlantic) disliked grits. They were a legitimate food group like chocolate and beer.

Mac, the owner and chef walked out and stared at her, wearing those silly checked chef pajama pants, an apron and a white tee-shirt. Sara thought he would probably be buried in that outfit.

Looking down at her 511 cargos, he noted "Awfully tactical looking today, there, Missy!"

"You caught me, Mac. I'm a Marine wannabe."

"You'd probably made a good jarhead. You are smart, strong and good-looking like me." He flexed the faded and stretched Marine Corps insignia tattoo on his bicep, now with loose skin where there had probably been significant muscle thirty years ago.

"I'll take that as a compliment, Mac! And, you are good-looking as hell. If you weren't seventy-five and happily married to the cashier and real boss of this café, I would be coming after you with a vengeance!"

He winked at her and said, "Nothing hotter than a woman with a gun!" She gave him her Wonder Woman smile and he walked back to the kitchen with a bit of spring to his step.

Sara finished her breakfast and hoped she could keep it down after watching the autopsy. Lynn thought autopsies were just interesting scientific, forensic exercises on "subjects." Sara guessed that was her way of compartmentalizing using a scalpel and a saw, and analyzing a vagina for signs of rape, and looking at stomach contents. "Okay, enough! No more, or Mac is not going to think you'd be a good Marine if you hurl and chase off his customers."

She walked up to the cashier with her check and credit card.

"You know? You are so blessed to have that big Marine!"

"Honey, we don't serve alcohol here and I didn't see you smoking the stuff I used to smoke when I wore tie-dyed undershirts. That was before my tits pointed at my toes, of course. This is just you and me talking. He is lucky to have me. He talks a good game, but I can chase him around the bed and catch him every time. Then, I have my way with him, whether he wants to or not!"

There really was not a response that Sara could come up with quickly, so she tried another smile and added a wink for good measure. It seemed to have communicated something that satisfied her co-conspirator, so she left while she was ahead.

******

At the morgue, Sara took the victim's fingerprints before the process started. She verified Lynn's original contention that there was no flesh under the fingernails, nor were there any defensive wounds on her arms or body. A magnified view of the wound supported use of a thin, sharp instrument, probably a razor, having been used to cut the victim's throat and cause her to die from sufficient exsanguination to cause death. There was no sign of recent sexual activity, even to the extent of prophylactic lubricant. The time of death was closely estimated to between eleven and one on Friday night. The victim was in excellent health and physical condition, was not pregnant and had a high alcohol content.

"Lynn, can you check the blood for Rohypnol or GNB. I will want to know if a date rape drug was used on her," Sara said.

"Not much use, honey. Both cease to show up in tests after 8-12 hours, GNB maybe sooner. Finding even a tiny bit would be a stretch."

"Go ahead and run it anyway. I have exactly zip on this one. I will take a stretch at this point."

"You got it," Lynn said as she drew two vials of blood from the deceased's arm.

"So, let me get this straight, Lynn. Someone she knew came in, she was enticed by the person or herself, to strip naked, but she did not have sex. Then, the person turned her head away to keep from getting sprayed with blood, and slit her throat? Then he wiped the place down and walked out unseen?"

"That's pretty much the sum of it, Sara."

"I don't have much to work on here, unless a roofie shows up."

"Nope."

"Sucks."

"Yep."

"Is this monosyllabic thing new?"

"Yep." After which, Lynn burst into laughter. "Gotcha for the stone face last night!"

"I'd hug you, but you have yuck all over your PPE."

Lynn looked at her quizzically.

"Personal protective equipment in first responder terms."

"I knew that, damn it! It's why anyone would not want to hug me that I cannot get past."

Sara took out her smart phone and took a quick picture before Lynn could avoid it.

She flipped the image around. "See? You look like something from a vampire movie."

"I'll remember that next time I fix grouper en Papillote."

"In that case, let me assure you that you look stunning."

"Too little, too late. You are hereby Papillote-less."

"Okay. I'll cook next time. See ya. Got people to question and crimes to solve."

"Give my best to that little shit that slugged his wife yesterday, okay?"

"Maybe I'll just give him the picture I just took."

"Do that! Tell him I'll be much yuckier after his autopsy!"

"Deal!"

CHAPTER 3

Sara walked into the courtroom at the circuit court and took a seat. She had a leather folio with the arrest report in it. She recognized some of the witnesses from the park, both family members and other unrelated park users who had watched transfixed as events had unfolded.

The suspect was not sitting there with his wife, whose jaw had some sort of wire thing holding it shut. In Florida, he could not have bonded out until a court appearance. Yet, unless she was a witness against him, she was there supporting the man who had dislocated her jaw and knocked out a tooth. People were weird. Relationships were weirder. Sara was glad that she had Lynn as a friend. The only understanding that they had was that they had no understanding. Friends with benefits. The ideal scenario that most guys dreamed about, and Sara had.

"All rise! The District Circuit Court is now in session, the Honorable Judge James Howard presiding."

Several cases where brought before the judge. He fined and jailed all defendants. Sara watched the wife's face drop lower each time someone got jail time.

His case was called. He was brought out in an orange jump suit. The charges against him were Domestic Battery and Resisting Arrest with Violence. The former was an upper level misdemeanor, the latter a felony punishable by both prison time and fines.

The man, Henry Sumter, was represented by counsel, who responded to the plea question with "not guilty." The assistant state's attorney called Sara first and the bailiff swore her in.

"For the court, please state your name and occupation."

Properly turning to the judge, Sara said: "Sara Lee Nichols, Detective with the Osprey County Sheriff's Office."

"Detective Nichols, how long have you been a detective?"

"I have been a detective with the Sheriff's Office for four years. For six years prior to that, I was a special agent with the Naval Criminal Investigative Service, or NCIS, so I guess I have been an investigator for ten years."

"Please tell the court what occurred at three thirty yesterday at Palmetto Creek Park."

"A friend and I had just finished kayaking the Calusa Blueway. We were putting our kayaks on top of our vehicles when I heard an argument getting louder and louder. I looked towards the sound and saw a subject strike a female with his fist, knocking her down. I retrieved my ID, sidearm and handcuffs and walked towards where they were located."

"What happened then, Detective?"

"I identified myself as a detective with the Sheriff's Office and had my ID plainly visible around my neck. I told him that I had observed him strike the female and that I was placing him under arrest for domestic battery."

"Is the person who struck the female in this courtroom?"

Sara turned and pointed to the defendant, saying "Yes, the defendant."

"And, the victim, Detective?"

"Yes, sir. The lady" pointing at her," with the wire device on her dislocated jaw."

"Objection!" the defense counsel yelled, "does the Detective have a medical degree that enables her to diagnose the injury?"

"Your Honor, the friend who was with me and called 911 is the County Medical Examiner. She is a physician and told me that she examined the victim and that the victim had lost one tooth and sustained a dislocated jaw."

The judge rapped his gavel and said "Overruled!"

"Detective, what happened after you advised the defendant he was under arrest?"

"He attacked me, by rushing at me with his head lowered for a butting attack."

"What happened then?"

"I knocked him down."

There was some laughter in the courtroom and the judge rapped his gavel again, though not as loudly as before.

"Then, Detective?"

"He got up and charged me again, so I kicked him in the groin and gave him a knife edge hand chop behind the neck. I then assumed a handcuffing position. As I was handcuffing him, he resisted. Several of his male friends or relatives came forward to assist him. I held up my hand and warned them back. They continued to come towards me in an aggressive manner. So, I drew my weapon and held them at gunpoint. The ME immediately advised 911 that the situation had escalated to an 'officer needs assistance' call. During this time, the ME motioned the victim over and began to diagnose her wounds. She then called for paramedics."

"Nothing further, Your Honor," the prosecutor said.

The defense counsel walked up to the witness stand.

"Detective Nichols, how were you dressed at the time this all occurred?"

"I was kayaking, so I was wearing a bathing suit with a tee shirt over top. Before intervening, I put this," she held up for the Court's review," laminated ID badge on this clearly marked Osprey Sheriff's Office lanyard, around my neck."

"So, you held up a tiny card that could have said anything and expected the defendant to be assured you were a law enforcement officer from merely that?"

"Counselor, I was about as far away from him as I am right now from you. I believe you can read the badge and I know you can read the "SHERIFF'S OFFICE" wording on the lanyard."

"So, a woman in a bathing suit with a lanyard she could have gotten anywhere and an unreadable plastic card approached the defendant and started yelling orders. Is that pretty much the sum of it?"

"No, counselor, that is pretty much a total misrepresentation of the facts."

The judge spoke: "Defense counsel and prosecutor will approach the bench."

"Might I remind you, counselor, that you are not playing a role for a jury here. I am the sole discretionary person in this matter. I cannot be swayed by false premises and would ask that you save innuendoes and drama for elsewhere."

"Yes, your honor."

Sara was excused and several non-associated witnesses testified, validating her recounting of events. The emergency room physician who had treated Mrs. Sumter testified about the extent of her injuries.

The judge declared a fifteen-minute recess, during which he met with the defense and prosecution.

Upon reconvening, he asked the defense if there was any change in their plea. The defense counsel, in a more subdued tone said "Yes, your Honor. The defendant wishes to change his plea to guilty on both charges."

The judge, expecting the change, waited a moment, then read his verdict and sentence.

"On the charge of Resisting Arrest with Violence, I find the Defendant guilty and sentence him to twenty-four months in state prison, with twelve months suspended. As to the Domestic Battery charge, I reduce that to misdemeanor Domestic Abuse and suspend sentencing. However, probation is contingent upon the Defendant taking a one-week course against battering when he gets out of prison. Mr. Sumter, do you understand this finding?"

The Defendant nodded.

"Excellent! One further thing, Mr. Sumter. If I see you in this court again for a similar charge, you can rest assured that I will not be so kind in my judgment as I have been today and I will impose the twelve months for the domestic charge that I suspended in addition to any subsequent charges."

"Bailiff, take the Defendant into custody and remand him over to the care of the Florida Department of Corrections." He struck his gavel and got up and left without further ado.

The Defendant turned and glared at Sara, as if it were all her fault. She smiled sweetly at him and turned and walked out of the door, something he would not have the joy of doing for at least a year.

******

Sara drove to the clothing store where Mary Ann Hixon had worked. While the owner wanted both her and her other employee to be interviewed at the same time, Sara did not allow that. Too much room for influence and "herd" effect. She took the owner first, jotting notes as she questioned and listened.

"Ms. Kilgallen, did Ms. Hixon ever mention anyone threatening her---an ex-boyfriend? Ex-husband? No? How about a stalker?"

"No, detective. Mary Ann never talked about her love life. Not to me, at least. I respected her privacy and gave her whatever space she needed."

Sara thought to herself, "Very nice of you. Doesn't help my solving this case by one shit, though. Wished you'd been the busy-body you probably wanted to be," but nodded supportively and listened further.

"She was an ideal employee. Always on time, never complained, the customers loved her."

"Did she ever mention anything odd from her past?"

"No, never. She actually didn't talk that much."

"Please take my card and call me if you remember anything, no matter how small."

The woman took the card and Sara summoned the other employee into the business office.

Sara stuck out her hand, "Hi, Detective Sara Nichols."

The other woman responded "Sophia Heyward."

"Ms. Hayward, what can you tell me about Ms. Hixson's social life?"

"We never went out. It was like a preference thing."

"So, Ms. Hixon was gay?"

"I got that vibe. She was down-low about it, but it was there if you looked for it."

"Did she ever mention anyone she was dating?"

"No, she never 'fessed up to being a lesbian to me."

"Were you good friends?"

"No, I don't think she actually had any close friends."

"Did she ever mention where she went for fun? Clubs or anything?"

"Yes and no. She said Friday that she was going 'up' to a club she liked. I figured it might be Ft. Myers. If there are any lesbian clubs between here and there, I haven't heard of them."

"That's very good information. Anything else?"

"Nope. That's about it."

She proffered her card and left.

A good lead, indeed! She knew of several clubs that would fit the bill in Ft. Myers. The victim could have driven past there and went to St. Petersburg or Tampa, but this would really narrow her search down. What she needed now was a pretty picture of Mary Ann Hixon to go with the shock shot from the morgue. She went to the house.

******

Hixson's parents from Jacksonville were there and were unable to get in the lock she had placed on the door. "All the better", Sara thought.

"Good morning. Are you the Hixson's? I am Detective Sara Nichols from the Osprey County Sheriff's Office. I am the lead investigator on this case. First off, I am very sorry for your loss. I will do everything humanly possible to find who did this and bring them to justice."

Mr. Hixson spoke. "How about giving me five minutes unattended with him?" She smiled.

"I wish I could. That might be the best justice of all. Unfortunately, our system of laws does not work that way."

"I cannot let you in; the apartment has not been cleaned yet and it's still a crime scene. Probably by tomorrow, you can get in."

"Detective, can you tell us what happened to our little girl?" the mother asked.

"There was no sign of forced entry or defensive wounds, which suggests that she knew and let in the attacker. She was killed with a sharp instrument. It appeared that she did not suffer and death was very fast."

"Was she raped?"

"No, that was completely negated by the autopsy. She was not."

"At least that…"

"Do either of you know anyone who had anything, no matter how small, against your daughter?"

Neither parent did.

"What can you tell me about her dating life? Who? Where did she meet people?"

The two looked at each other, the man giving the woman a look of warning that Sara picked up instantly.

"Mr. Hixson. We know about your daughter's preferences. Any information will help a lot, because there really isn't very much that has come to light yet," she said.

"I can see why a man would be disappointed that a beautiful girl like our daughter would not be interested in him? What I can't see is how he would get invited in here and then kill her," he questioned.

"That bothers me, too," Sara said. "And, I don't have an answer for it yet. But, I will. She clearly felt safe with this man. I guess it's possible she let someone in who subsequently left and another intruder came in through the unsecured doors, but there still should be defensive wounds..."

"We would help you if we could, but we are drawing a blank. And, we are still in shock over all of this," the mother said.

"Let me recommend that you find a specialty cleaning service and have them contact me to let them in. That way, when you come in to get your daughter's belongings, things will be back to normal."

******

After the Hixon's left, Sara went in and looked around for a picture. She found a five by seven glamour shot in a frame and took the picture out and placed it in the front of the case folder.

She went into the kitchen and stood. The blood was still on the floor, though just a thick darker mess now. Sara closed her eyes and visualized the night of the murder in her mind. Hixon enters with another person—now, it could be a female, though the US has had very few female serial killers—and undresses. She comes back into the kitchen. Sara concluded she undressed in her bedroom, since her clothes were hastily folded on the bed. She was wearing only jewelry and the knock-off Louboutin high heels, so she was dressed to entice. If Sophia was right, it might be a female, though in Sara's experience, unlikely. Maybe Sophia was wrong. Or, maybe Mary Ann Hixon was bisexual. Many gay women stayed at an arm's length from bi's. Too much chance of AIDS or some other disease from their activities with men. But, other lesbians were not so selective and were thinking good time instead of thinking about staying alive and or healthy. Maybe Hixon was one of those.

Sara had two lesbian clubs she wanted to visit just south of Ft. Myers. But, it would not do much good to visit them until after dark. She would want to get the proper shift of bartenders and servers...and, maybe customers and murderers present.

For the rest of the day, she did follow-ups on another case in her caseload. It was a rape that had occurred on the beach. It was two adults. One claimed consent, the other claimed she did not give consent. It was reported almost immediately and the rape kit confirmed sex. The interview of both confirmed that they each had had copious amounts of alcohol also. So, it was basically a "he said, she said" situation. Sara had to go forward on the premise that rape had occurred and let the chips fall where they might.

She had obtained witness information from the beach-front bar where they had dinner and drinks. It would be helpful to know whether they were romantic, argumenta-tive, or what? Not conclusive, just helpful.

Sara waited until four and went to the bar, knowing that was when the bartender who served them came on duty.

"Shawn? I'm Detective Nichols. We spoke earlier."

"Oh, yeah. Hi. What can I do for you?"

"Do you recognize either or both of these two people? They were supposedly in here and ate at the bar on Thursday night. I guess you have been out of town since."

"Yeah, I was at a wedding in New York. Let me look closer at the pictures. Yeah. I remember them. Started off kinda lovey-dovey. By the end of the night, were at each other's throats."

"How were they when they left?"

"Apart! I called a cab for her. And, she went off in it. He stayed a little longer until I cut him off the booze. Then, he left."

"What cab company do you use?"

"Veteran's. Here's the number." He wrote it on a cocktail napkin.

"About what time did she leave by cab?"

"I'm thinking around eleven, give a take fifteen minutes either way."

"Thanks, Shawn. That helps a lot."

"You bet. What's this all about?"

"I really can't say. But, again, thanks."

Sara went out to the Charger and dialed the cab company on her smart phone.

"Hi. This is Detective Nichols with the Osprey Sheriff's Office. I need to find out about a taxi that responded to the Blue Gull Bar on Thursday night."

"You gotta come by with some ID to get that, okay?"

"Yes. Makes sense. Give me your address." He did and she promised to be there in ten minutes. She made it in eight.

Sara got buzzed in. The dispatcher scrutinized her badge and ID, notwithstanding the golf shirt and black gun she was wearing.

He looked in a computer and after a couple of minutes said, "Got it! Taxi 17 picked up a fare and took her to this address." He wrote the address and gave it to her.

"Is the driver on now? Yes? Can you get him to swing by here so I can talk with him?"

"Yep, but it's a 'her. Bertha. Tough lady!"

"Taxi 17? Respond back her to talk with somebody, okay?"

"She will be here directly."

"Thanks for your help. I will go out and meet her."

"It's a Crown Vic. Old cop car. "

"Thanks. I will watch for it."

Sara went out. Presently, an old Ford sedan painted as a Veteran's Cab appeared. The woman behind the wheel was large and very serious looking.

Sara said "Bertha?"

"Yeah, that's me."

"You picked up a white female at the Blue Gull bar on Thursday night around eleven and took her to Cape Coral to an apartment complex?"

"Hmm. I remember her. Drunk and pissed off at her boyfriend."

"Remember anything she said?"

"No exact words. Just the drift of it, ya know? She said he was a two-timing bastard. I told her most men were. She said she'd get his ass, one way or the other."

"What do you think she meant by that?"

"Don't know. Just took it at face value. Payback is a mutha and this lady looked like she was out to make this guy sorry for whatever he did."

"What happened when you got back to her apartment?"

"I had to help her up to the door and unlock it for her."

"Was it dark?"

"Yep. Nobody there."

Sara knew that the boyfriend was still drinking at the

Blue Gull at this time.

"Ya know what's funny, Detective?"

"No, what?"

"Ain't no such thing as a blue gull. Stupid ass name for a bar. There's a blue bird and a gray heron, but no blue gull."

"I've thought about that, too. Dumb, huh?"

"Yep."

"Thanks, Bertha. You be safe out here, huh?"

"You, too, honey."

Sara grinned at her and she drove off, the million-mile Crown Vic sounding pretty good.

She went back to the bar and timed the trip to the victim's apartment. She deducted five minutes due to her having more traffic than at the time of the taxi trip. She knew when the victim claimed her boyfriend had come back to her apartment and attacked her. It didn't fit. She called the victim. The victim did not answer, but Sara saw her car parked out front. She was at home, so Sara surprised her with a knock on her door.

"Oh! I guess that was you, just now?"

"It was. May I come in??

"Yes. Have you arrested Carlos yet?"

"No. Let's sit down."

They did and Sara began.

"You left the bar, and according to several witnesses were very inebriated. At the time you said Carlos was raping you, he was still at the bar. We know you had sex, but the when part is getting questionable. You told someone you were going to get even with him for two-timing you. You want to recant any of your claims now?"

The victim began to squirm and dig her bare toes into the carpet. She broke eye contact.

"I was tired, so I went to bed. I was sleeping well. Then, it was his fault! He woke me up and raped me. He's the bastard."

Sara recognized a word bridge between "I" and the shift to "his", which indicated she was probably now lying.

"You are not telling me the truth, Alicia. Making false statements to a police officer is illegal. What you are claiming that Carlos did is a serious crime. A felony punishable by a long prison sentence. If it ends up you stick with your lies and they are found to be such—and, I think they are lies—it could be you in prison, not Carlos. You would not do so well in prison, believe me."

Alicia broke down and began crying hysterically. Sara let her run through it to see if she was faking. She judged from the noise and profusion of water, either she was not faking or she was a world-class actress. Sara decided to go with the former.

After five minutes, Alicia brought her self under control. Sara had said nothing, knowing that silence on the part of an interrogator was a powerful tool, if used appropriately.

"Look me in the eye, Alicia."

The woman did, albeit hesitatingly.

"Carlos did not rape you, did he?"

She shook her head "no."

"The rape kit was positive. You had sex with somebody. Who and when?"

"The pool guy the next morning. I wanted to pay Carlos back for screwing around on me. But, I knew from TV about the rape kits, so I knew I needed some semen in me. The pool boy looked good and he was convenient, so I screwed his brains out and called 911 afterwards."

Sara considered the concept of safe sex but said nothing.

"You want to drop charges?"

"What happens if I don't?"

"It will be found out in court that you lied and you will be charged and Carlos freed."

"Can't that happen anyway?"

"It could. But, if you take this thing all the way, you *will* be charged and go to jail. The other way is up to the Assistant State's Attorney, not a Circuit Court judge who can sentence you to prison."

"Are you going to arrest me?"

"Not unless the Assistant State's Attorney tells me to."

"How do I drop the charges?"

"Come down to the courthouse with me right now and stand before a magistrate."

"I'll get my shoes and purse."

"Okay. I will be right here waiting."

CHAPTER 4

The timing of the recanting of charges worked out well for Sara. She had time to drive up to the Ft. Myers area and hit the two lesbian clubs.

Secretly, she hoped Carlos would sue the hell out of his now ex-girlfriend for slander. It was hard enough for women to break through a glass ceiling or even get by on an even keel. With women like Alicia, the rest took a step backwards with every false claim.

Sara decided to eat at the bar of the first one. Before leaving, she went into the locker room and changed into a golf shirt without a sheriff motif and to dark blue slacks. The Sig went into her briefcase and locked into the Charger's trunk. A small backup revolver was strapped to her left ankle and two six-shot strips of extra ammo went into her left pocket. She dropped the cuff of her slacks over the small gun and it disappeared.

While her carriage and often stern expression screamed "cop" to other cops and to criminals, she just looked like a really pretty woman of around forty to everyone else. She hoped that would be the case tonight. While she was not technically in the closet, she did not advertise Whatever her sexual orientation may be for professional reasons. It was just simpler and more fun to let folks wonder. Including perps. Hell, if she were straight, she would not have advertised that either.

She parked the obvious police Charger several blocks down from the first club and walked. She often had to spend too much time on her butt and enjoyed the exercise.

There were several open stools at the bar and she took one. The bartender asked what she wanted and she replied she wanted a menu and an unsweetened iced tea.

She got both and ordered a Cobb salad. Once it came she began to pick at it and deliberated about her questioning approach.

"You recognize this girl?" she asked the very butch bartender, as she put the photo down on the bar.

"What are you, some kind of private dick?"

"No, Osprey County detective."

"Why do you want to know?"

This one looked tough, so Sara decided to see how tough. She slid the autopsy facial picture over beside the glamour shot.

"I asked if you recognize her."

"Never seen her in my life."

"Look close and think about it. It's important."

"Nope. Never."

"You tend bar here Friday night?"

"Yep."

"Just you?"

"Yep."

Sara oriented her attention to her salad. As soon as she was done, she paid the bill and left with no further ado.

She had parked midway between the two clubs, so she walked past Argo and proceeded on to the other club.

Sara sat at the bar again. She ordered coffee. Black. This one had pretty bartender. Upon being presented the glamour shot, she showed recognition, but did not readily admit to it.

So, Sara handed her the autopsy shot. The woman shrank back from that one.

"Please tell me the truth this time. You may be a helluva bartender but you are a suck liar."

"She was here Friday. It was a bleak night for a Friday. She was the best-looking woman here. And, she left with the other best looking one. They sat over there," pointing to a table across from a small, now-vacant stage."

"Is she dead?"

"Yes."

"How did she die?"

"Somebody killed her. How did she and the other good looking one pay?"

"She paid by credit card, the other one by cash."

"Shit!" Sara thought. "What did the other one look like exactly?

"Almost your height with three-inch heels. Long blonde hair. Blue eyes. I'd do her."

"Nice figure?"

"Oh, yeah!"

"Name of the blonde?"

"Dunno."

"Who was their server?" Sara asked.

"Brenda?" the bartender responded.

"She here tonight?"

"Yes. That is her in the cut-offs, looking for the world like Daisy Duke."

"Will you get me a table in her section?" The bartender nodded affirmatively.

Sara paid for her cup of coffee and took it to the table. Still hungry, but conscious of her figure, she ordered a fruit cup for dessert from Brenda.

When Brenda came back, Sara said "Brenda, please sit for a second."

"I'll get in trouble if I do."

"With whom?"

"The manager. She's the one over there already glowering at me."

Sara caught the manager's eye and motioned her over. Brenda almost lost lunch.

"Is there a problem here?"

"Not at all. I am Detective Nichols from Osprey County. I am investigating a homicide. The victim was killed after leaving your club Friday night. I'd like to ask you and Brenda some questions."

"Why don't the three of us go into my office and you can show me some ID. We can talk there without attracting negative advertising."

"Great idea. Lead the way."

They entered the small office. Sara spied a Marine emblem. "Were you a WM?"

"I was a Woman Marine. Last duty was Master at Arms at Beaufort Naval Hospital."

"I worked with a lot of MAA's when I was an NCIS agent a few years ago."

"I always figured the NCIS and SEALS were the best of the swabbies."

"And, the Corpsmen!"

"Damn right!"

That bonding would facilitate the conversation to follow, Sara knew.

She produced the before and after photos for the manager, now identified as retired Gunnery Sergeant Helen Wright, to look at.

"Yes! She was in here Friday! Most of our clientele Friday looked like Chesty Puller instead of like her! She left with a looker though."

"Gunny, it's that looker I need to find and talk to. She

may be the last person Mary Ann Hixon ever spoke with."

"She was not the killer, right?"

"I doubt it, but I'd sure like to find out what she knows."

"Brenda: how'd she pay? "

"Cash, Boss."

"That doesn't help, does it Special Agent?"

"It's just detective now. But, you are right. A credit card would have been great. Brenda: did you hear her name?"

"It was loud with the band, but I think it might have been Ellie." Sara wrote that in her case notes.

"Please describe everything you can about her to me. Her height, weight, build, hair, eyes, voice, any accent."

"She was tall, almost like you, but not quite. Built about like you. Long blonde hair, blue eyes, nice tits, and a really sexy voice."

"Sexy how, Brenda?"

"Kinda slow and breathy. Definitely Southern. We get enough New Yorkers for me to recognize a fellow Southerner in a second."

"What did they eat and drink?"

"The dead girl had Lemmy's and the other had one or two glasses of white wine. That's all."

"Okay, what's a 'Lemmy?'" Sara asked.

"Jack and Coke."

"Oooh-kay. Many women here order that?"

"Not so much the fems like these two. They mostly stay with the wine, like the second one did.

"Would you say they were inebriated when they left?"

"The one who died certainly was," Brenda said with the Gunny nodding in support.

"The other?"

"She acted like it, but only had two glasses all night. She seemed pretty sober when she came in, too."

"So, maybe faking being drunk?"

"That's what I'd guess."

"Did either of them speak with anyone else?"

"I didn't see them talk with anyone but me."

"How would you characterize their conversation with each other and with you?"

"With each other, it was definitely, let's blow this joint and hop in bed. With me, it was more booze for the dead one, not much from the other."

"You didn't happen to see any cars associated with them did you?"

"No, I didn't."

"Thanks, Brenda and Gunny. You guys have been a big help."

"Is this the girl from the paper who got her throat cut?"

"I really can't comment on that," Sara said, shaking her head affirmatively.

The former Gunny smiled at her; Brenda shivered and Sara left, deeply in thought.

"If you discount Lizzie Borden and her ax and its whacks," Sara thought to herself as she drove down Rt. 41, the Tamiami Trail, "Florida had executed one of the rare well-known female serial killers in US history, but there had been as many as thirty-eight operating during the same period in the US alone. And," she thought further, "a blade is more of a woman's weapon than a man's. Men like to shoot people. But, I still think it is highly likely that it's a man. She might have left with the blonde, but I doubt that's who killed her."

As she was thinking about this, the car's radio grabbed her attention.

"Unit 4029, respond to parking lot of the Publix Supermarket on Cross Winds Drive off Rt. 41 on a homicide."

"4029 responding from Ft. Myers."

She grabbed her phone from her belt clip and called

dispatch. "What's the nature of this one?"

"Female. Throat cut. This time looks like from all the blood reported, it must have happened in her car at Publix."

"Copy. Got a sergeant, CSI and the ME on the way?"

"10-4. We just got it. A kid clearing baskets for the supermarket found her."

"I'll run hard, but I am a way off yet."

"10-4. Crowd is gathering, so run at your discretion."

Sara hit the wig-wag headlights and the red and blue high intensity flashing LED lights in her windshield and back window. There was some traffic, so she touched the "yelp" button on the siren whenever someone was reticent about moving aside. That tended to work.

As she got in hearing distance, she turned off the siren, but kept her foot well into the big engine. She pulled into the lot and doused her lights. She immediately saw a black Expedition and said, "Shit!"

It was her sheriff, Rob Roy MacNab. She loved him. He was not Joe Arpaio, Grady Judd, Wayne Ivey or David Clarke, but he certainly was at least on the second tier of great sheriffs of America behind those great guys...at least in her book. But, his presence meant politics and media coverage. The media loved him, with his Southern good ole boy charm and faint Scot accent from forty years ago. He was a force to be reckoned with by anyone. Luckily, he thought the world of her and she of him. But, him being there on scene was guaranteed to complicate things.

She walked up to a yellow Mustang just as the television trucks pulled into the lot, ahead of the crime scene van and the ME.

"Hi, Boss!"

"Sara, looks like we got another young female with her throat slashed. I read your report on the first one. This looks, at first glance, to be similar. The media people pulling in already are gonna yell "serial killer." We gotta be ahead of all that. This could hurt tourism. That could hurt lots of things."

"I know, Sheriff. I am just back from some good leads on the first case—the Hixon one. I would like to get an artist as soon as I can for a sketch to show the people inside the store. There will be a lot more people this time to interview, too."

"You lemme know what you want, Sara, and you got it."

"Thanks, I will."

She grabbed the first deputy she saw and asked him to point out the basket boy who found the victim. He did and she asked that he be escorted into the store and the manager asked to gather his or her employees.

Sara looked into the Mustang. There was blood everywhere. She put on blue nitrile gloves and removed the victim's purse. She took out the driver's license and placed the purse in her car trunk. "Alana Morton" was the name. Age thirty-eight. Single. Five foot eight. Looking at the body instead of the driver's license, Sara characterized her as slightly plumb, but not at all obese. She was looking at a Mary Ann Hixon situation all over again, just dressed this time. That, she thought, is a very bad sign. It signaled a frenzy or panic attack kill, instead of a planned one. The only good aspect was maybe, just maybe, mistakes were made.

The CSI's had erected a tarp framework and powerful lights around the car, enabling them to work both efficiently and in total privacy from the public and the media. A deputy was left there to keep the media from violating that privacy. Sara had marshalled the efforts of the other deputies to help inside the store.

"Hello, everyone. I am Detective Sara Nichols with the Osprey Sheriff's Office. We have, as you probably know, had a homicide in the parking lot. The deputies or I will need to speak briefly to each of you. I would ask this, based on 'way too many years of conducting interviews like this: first, do not compare notes. We need to get your uncorroborated version of what you saw. Second, tell us everything. What may be unimportant could be the one thing that solves the case. Okay? Now, one thing I want you to focus on. Did you see a tall, pretty woman with long blonde hair either with the victim or in the area? She is a person of interest—not a suspect. She may be a friend of the victim who got scared and ran off. But, we need to talk with her."

"The person I am calling the 'victim' is a white female, tall, very voluptuous and with blondish hair. The sooner we can get this done, the sooner everyone gets to go home, whether you work here or are customers."

It took Sara and the deputies and one arriving sergeant two hours to finish interviewing everyone. Ten percent of the people saw the attractive victim in the store. Zero percent saw the person of interest. But, the best thing that she learned from the manager was that, due to some strong-armed robberies in the parking lot, they had put in surveillance cameras. Sara, immediately upon learning this, had a CSI take custody of the DVD for the current day. She also asked that the previous day and Friday be obtained. She wanted to make sure there was no photo of Mary Ann Hixon on Friday's recording.

Midway in the questioning, Sara had walked out to the crime scene between interviews. Lynn was there and had determined the time of death to be only an hour before and the cause of death to be bleeding to death because of severed carotid artery and jugular vein.

Lynn had leaned closely to Sara and said in a low voice, "I suspect the perp got some blood on himself this time. It is highly unlikely that he was in the back seat of the car. I did some reconstructions on the Friday murder. He has to be at least five-eleven, based on the angle of the slice. I just don't see someone that tall hoping in and out of that little thing Ford sells as a back seat in the Mustang, do you?" Sara nodded in agreement.

"Also, tests came back. No date rape drugs, but a concentration of cocaine. I still think she operating at full capacity though, alcohol notwithstanding."

"Thanks. Your office at nine in the morning?"

"You got it."

"See ya. Thanks for the good info."

"We serve and protect. No, wait a minute. That's you. We slice and dice."

Sara shook her head at her friend's macabre sense of humor and walked off.

******

The man in the van sat parked in the dark in the supermarket parking lot, observing. He monitored the scrambled or "coded" police channel on a scanner that had been programmed to override the security. He learned all he needed to know for now and slowly pulled out before anyone noticed him.

******

At the end of the interviews, Sara went to the address on the victim's driver's license. It was an apartment. She knocked on the door with the strong "cop knock" she had perfected over the years.

A sleepy-looking brunette in nothing but a very thin tee shirt came to the door. She was quite attractive.

"I am Detective Sara Nichols. Are you Alana Morton's roommate?"

"Yes, is something wrong?"

"I'd better come in, and you should take seat so we can talk."

Once inside and seated on the sofa in a slightly messy apartment, Sara re-introduced herself and asked the room-mate's name.

"I'm Sally Henson. I just woke up with the knock on the door. Alana's supposed to be here. I was asleep last night and heard her say she was gonna run out for some groceries. Where is she?"

"Sally, I'm afraid I have bad news for you. Alana died tonight. She was murdered in the Publix parking lot. I am sorry for your loss and need to get information from you about her next of kin."

Sally Henson lost it completely and broke into tears, rocking back and forth on the sofa sobbing.

Sara got up and went into the bathroom and unrolled a foot or two of toilet paper and brought it back for her. She took it and blew her nose loudly.

She gave her a couple more minutes to regain some composure, then asked her a question.

"Can I assume your relationship went beyond just being roommates?"

"Yes, we are…were…lovers," Sally sobbed and broke down again.

"I need to ask you some questions while the trail is still warm, okay? You do want the person caught quickly?"

"Of course! I want his thing cut off and shoved down his throat!"

"How do you know it was a 'he?'"

"It always is! Men are …" she trailed off trying to think of the worst thing she could use to describe men.

"Was anyone mad with her? Had Alana had any dis-agreements with anyone recently?"

"No. Never. Everyone loved her."

"Do either of you know a tall, pretty blonde? Almost my height."

"Alana said she had met someone up in Ft. Myers who was pretty cool and that I'd like her, too. She was going to invite her to dinner to see what would happen."

"Did you guys swing a little?"

"Is that against the law?"

"No. But knowing it would be a lead I could work on to maybe prevent the next girl from getting killed."

"Maybe a little."

"Do you remember a name, or phone number for this person?"

"No. Alana was going to take care of it. I was going to cook. That's why she went to the supermarket last night. To buy food. Dinner was going to be tomorrow—no, I guess now, it would be tonight—at seven."

Before following the logical line of questioning further, Sara asked one question before she forgot it: "Which club in Ft. Myers was the one where Alana met this blonde?" The answer was the one where Sara had just been. "When was that?"

"I think yesterday afternoon. Alana was working up there selling water softening services and stopped in for lunch. She bumped into her then. The blonde seemed receptive for a little visit, so..."

"Look, Sally. This person is a person of interest, not a suspect. If she doesn't know Alana is dead, she will probably still come for dinner. Why don't you plan on that? The groceries are all bad in the back of Alana's car now, so you can't use those. If she shows up unaware and you don't have dinner ready, that's surely plausibly deniable under the circumstances. I'd like to be here at seven to see if she arrives, okay?"

"Uh...okay, I guess."

"Now, do you have contact information for Alana's family?"

"Yeah. Let me go get it. You can come too, if you want."

Sara followed her into the bedroom, where she logged onto a computer and pulled up "contacts." She copied, pasted and printed the contact information for John and Hanna Morton of Hagerstown, Maryland. Sara called the office and had a notification of next of kin fax sent to the Hagerstown Police Department. She slipped the printed page into her new Alana Morton case file.

Sara questioned Sally for another thirty minutes. The young woman was both bright and very attractive. She and Alana, more from the picture she had gotten from Sally than from seeing her briefly dead in the car, suggested they were a hot, good-looking couple.

The most obvious thing that Sara observed, but did not comment upon, was the similarity between Alana, and the first victim, Mary Ann. Both were tall, buxom and had light reddish blonde hair. That seemed a coincidence. She would bet there would be a third victim, and that she would meet a similar description. Sara knew there were virtually no coincidences in police work.

CHAPTER 5

The new Crime Analyst was due in today, since the clock had already eclipsed midnight, and there was a meeting of all members of the Investigative Division at three. The lieutenant, an investigative assistant who did miscellaneous clerical duties, the two CSI teams and the several detectives were it, until now. Now, the much-needed analyst was filling out a very good team. Lt. Jaime "Jim" Gonzalez had cut his investigative teeth on the mean streets of Miami-Dade; he was a fair and competent leader and respected by all.

Sara went home, took care of the two cats and took a three-hour nap. After, she put on a pretty blouse that buttoned up the front and coordinating slacks. She put the ankle holster with the Kimber revolver on and stuck the badge clip on the waistband and her handcuffs in pants pockets. She was going to portray a friend of Alana's and Sally's in five hours and wanted to look like something other than a cop. She put on makeup and fixed her hair instead of the usual ponytail. As she looked in the mirror, she thought that the first almost forty years had been very good to her. She looked good, she thought. Damned good.

Sara went to the county morgue by eight forty-five in the morning to meet Lynn for Alana's autopsy. It was pretty straightforward. A right-handed person had slit her throat, just like in the first case. Lynn was unable to tell if the person was taller, as in the first case, because blood evidence had indicated she had died inside the car, behind the wheel. Since there was no blood splatter to the passenger side, the attacker was likely in the back seat. Again, there was no sign of defensive injuries or flesh under the fingernails that could be used for DNA identification or evidence of presence. Alana showed mild alcohol in her system. It was far too little, given her size, to suggest she was at all hampered by it. There was no indication of drugs. A height and weight comparison between the two victims was within three pounds and one inch.

Lynn chastised Sara as she was wrapping up the autopsy. "I will have the report ready by this afternoon. But, you have to stop this stuff! Somebody is killing some of the best-looking lesbians in Osprey County. These are not hookers. They are nice, hot girls. So, get on it, hot rod! Solve the case. Do it now!"

Sara responded, "But, how do you really feel, Lynn?"

"Frustrated, honey."

"Me, too."

Just before three, Sara filled her NCIS mug with the fourth cup of java for the day and strolled in. Everybody but the lieutenant, generally referred to as "LT," and the analyst were there.

Detective Bob Axelrod had his chair leaned back precipitously and the left boot of a pair of ostrich cowboy boots showing prominently.

"New boots, Bob? Must be! Otherwise, you would not be putting your ass at such risk of getting cracked again by falling backwards off the chair just to make sure we see them. Very nice! Now straighten up. You are making me nervous."

"Aha! The sweet and lovely Detective Nichols has arrived. At least, I think that is my friend Sara with the fancy hair and makeup. Thank you, Sara. I am so fricking glad you noticed my new boots. Just think if you had had a pair with these pointy toes, the damage you could have done to that wife-beater you kicked in the crotch Sunday! Since a kick in the nuts is not official police close combat policy, I am thinking it was some kind of womanly retribution, huh?"

Sara had taken a seat, took a sip of coffee and smiled sweetly. She blew him a kiss, causing Detective Cynthia Leton to wink and clap her hands soundlessly.

"Okay, enough of this inter-office romance!" Lt. Jim Gonzalez walked in grinning and was followed by a woman with thick curly dark hair and in a wheelchair.

"I'm gonna introduce our new crime analyst and then want you-all to go around the table and introduce yourselves."

"This is Maura Kelton. She comes to us from the east coast of Florida, where she was an analyst for five years with Brevard County SO. She has three degrees from the University of South Florida, terminating with a doctorate. She has contributed to the closure and successful prosecution of some of the highest profile cases in the Melbourne area. I am really excited to have stolen her and think she is going to be an immediate and major asset to Osprey County SO. Maura, you and Sara should talk about your pre-law enforcement jobs as professional athletes. She was a pro-beach volleyball player and Maura was a pro-golfer on the LPGA."

Everyone introduced themselves, each welcoming the analyst. Afterwards, the LT called for a quick case review. He held Sara for last.

"Sara: breeze through the rape case and get to the two murders. They have become hot topics and the media is already hinting about a serial killer at work."

"Okay, Boss. I got the 'victim' to admit that the charge of rape against her now-ex boyfriend was payback. She had a positive rape kit, but the pool boy had contributed to that effort the next morning. The dumb girl has never heard of either safe sex or DNA, I guess. I took her to the magistrate and she dropped charges."

"Is the Assistant State's Attorney going to charge her?"

"I don't think so. Ashley Jackson was going to have the case. She suggested, that while no hard and fast decision had been made yet, her inclination was not to load the criminal docket up with stuff like this, but to let the boyfriend pursue it civilly if he wanted."

"Good work! Now, the murders please. Everybody put your thinking caps on, this is probably going to become a team effort with Sara as lead. Maura, this will definitely be your first priority," the lieutenant said.

"Quick summary: we have had two strawberry blondes, both attractive, have their throats cut by an unknown assailant. It appears that both were gay and I have tracked down that both were at a Ft. Myers lesbian club before being murdered. The murderer was taller, at least that is shown in the first incidence, and was right-handed. He used a straight razor or similar very sharp, non-serrated blade. There is a tall, blonde female who was present at the club, she made contact with both vics, and is a person of interest. She was supposed to have dinner with the second victim and her lover tonight at seven. I will be there to see if she shows. I don't think she's going to be the killer, but I want to talk with her anyway. The two blondes have no connection except for her and the club, hence she is a POI."

"Maura—and maybe Cindy and Bob—where I really could use some more eyes is on the Publix parking lot surveillance film. I need to see if the Person of Interest is in them and is interacting outside the car with the victim."

Maura spoke. "Two vics do not a serial killer make... yet, anyway. But, that they are both gay, have a common POI, and look alike really pushes things toward that conclusion. The FBI has a wonderful database called VICAP, for Violent Criminal Apprehension Program. It is sadly under-contributed to by state and local agencies. We should all be dumping as much into it as we can. But, I'd like to run what we've got on this and see what the folks at the Critical Incident Response Group, or CIRG, that run it, can offer. That same group houses the profiler teams, so we might get some help there, too. I will get the tapes from you guys after you look at them," she said to the CSI teams. "After all, you saw the victim firsthand and know the positioning and description of the car, so you would be faster in setting up the situation to scrutinize."

"Great idea, Maura," Gonzalez said, "and Sara, take Cynthia with you tonight. She can pretend to be your date or something, since it's a gay dinner. Call the effort 'under cover.' I know you like to work on your own, but we are dealing with a killer who is good enough to not leave any clues. I feel in my bones that you and your team are going to find that this isn't his first rodeo. So, I want redundancy. Got it?"

"10-4, LT!"

Detective Axelrod opened his mouth, but seeing the glares from his two fellow detectives, wisely decided that discretion was truly the better part of valor.

"Sure we don't need SWAT?" Bob Axelrod asked seriously, obviously a thought other than the one he had been about to share. "This guy has killed two people. Even if it's a woman, and this woman in particular, we have to assume she is armed and very dangerous."

"Bob, I see your point, but here's how we can do this: I will wear a wire and maybe you can come to monitor it and be backup. We'll work out a panic word and you come through the unlocked doors and be our cavalry. I really am looking at this woman as a common denominator, not a suspect. But, just among the team, I fear we have a serial killer, no matter whether male or female."

The Lieutenant was watching her carefully as she spoke and considering every word. "Sara, I tend to lean with your call. Just be careful and remember our Kevlar vests don't work against blades, only bullets. Bob, are you available tonight?" The big detective nodded affirmatively.

"I am, LT. I doubt she's going to show. By now, enough information has been broadcast on the news to scare her off. That's a shame, because she met both victims at the same gay bar on the same day. That's a really big coincidence in my book!" Axelrod said.

Cindy Leton spoke up: "When do you want Bob and me and what's the address? I have a couple of things to do first."

"Why not six o'clock at this address", tearing off two partial sheets form her notebook and passing them to the two other Osprey detectives.

"Cool. I'll be there." Cindy said.

"Me, too." Bob added.

"Sara, do you have time to review the actual case file with me?" Maura asked.

"Sure, let's stay in here unless someone else has the conference room booked.

"It's not, you can stay," Mary Higgins, the investigative assistant said.

"Maura, move over here, if you would. I have everything out already.

She moved the wheelchair around the conference table to Sara's side and took out a notebook from a pouch in the side.

The others left and Sara spoke.

"First off, welcome aboard again! I am really glad you're here. We all are!"

"Thanks. It was hard to leave Brevard, but I was able to kill two birds with one stone."

"How's that?"

"A teaching job several nights a week at Florida Gulf Coast University nearby. It will keep the juices flowing and increase my income by about forty percent."

"That's great! So you were on the LPGA circuit?"

"I was! I was not great, but was having fun and earning an increasing amount of money every year. Then, this happened," gesturing down to her wheelchair.

"What was the 'this,' if you don't mind me asking?"

"You know how they say there is 'no such thing as a minor motorcycle accident? Well, in this case, the famous and often wrong 'they' were right."

"Tough break."

"It was, but, if there was a silver lining, it was going back to school and focusing on something I had always been interested in. Now, I think I make a difference... before, I think I just made money."

"I feel the same way; the pro beach volleyball was a blast, though the money was not there. But, I didn't make a difference either. At NCIS, and now here, I do."

"NCIS is pretty hot stuff. Why from there to here?"

"It's a great service, though nothing like the three TV shows at all. I was sent all over the world at their whim. I was in Afghanistan and Iraq several times in combat zones. I didn't like the military's way of hiding domestic abuse and other things by not sharing with civilian law enforcement, even the NCIC. Many times since, I have worked cases on people with no known criminal histories to find they had lengthy and violent rap sheets in the military. And, then, I missed home in Florida. So, I started looking and came within thirty miles of where I was born and raised. Win-win!"

"Do you have a family, Sara?"

"I do. I have parents and a slightly younger brother who is thirty-six. He is married and has two kids that I adore."

"No significant other?"

"Not right now. Maybe one day. I'm too busy and having too much fun to get caught up in relationships now. How about you?"

"A husband. We met after the accident. He's really good about my challenges and about everything else."

"What does he do?"

"He's a FedEx guy. So, he was able to transfer over with me without any trouble or losing any seniority."

"That's great, Maura. Back to the case, before I have to go and grab the wire gear. Here is what I have so far. Here a crime scene pictures and autopsy pictures and report on the first case."

Twenty minutes of discussion later, Sara asked "What is your gut so far?"

"I'm with you one hundred percent. This is going to be serial, with the same modus operandi, sexual preference, and the striking similarity in the looks of the victims. I lean towards a male perp, too. The POI female will surely have something that will help, but what that is up in the air. What I'd like to do, Sara, is reach out to VICAP this afternoon while you are gearing up to meet the person of interest. Let's see if they have anything on similar crimes, okay?"

"Sounds like a plan! If you get a hit, and I am already gone, take my card and text it to the cell number on the card."

"Copy that. Let's get this bastard!"

Sara smiled and winked at Maura. "We will. You can take that to the bank."

******

By prior agreement, Sara showed up at Sally's apartment in her orange Jeep Wrangler. Cindy, whose police vehicle was a blue Impala, parked one street over and walked to the address. Bob drove a white Tahoe. Though it looked like a police vehicle, it was plausible that at least one deputy or officer might live in the complex, so he parked ten spaces down. The three met inside the apartment, after Sara had done a surveillance ride-through and given the others the all-clear call via cell phone. In character, she and Cindy arrived together in the Jeep and carried a couple of plastic grocery bags in. But, instead of gift snacks or wine, one had the wire equipment, and the other had snacks.

"Sally, this is Detective Cynthia Leton. If the blonde person actually shows and comes in, just introduce me as your neighbor Sara and Cindy as my friend."

"Wow, Sara. You look different! I didn't realize your hair was that long."

"I do it in a bun or ponytail or French braid to keep it out of the way when I'm working. Would you show Cindy how to get out of your back patio, so the backup detective can meet her back there and get set up?"

Sally led Cindy to the rear of the apartment and Sara heard the patio door off the kitchen open. She went into the bathroom with the wire equipment and closed the door only partially, as she knew Bob would probably not come in. He had to get set up to monitor her wire and rush in if the right word was uttered.

Sara took off her blouse and the thin cami to attach the wire. She heard a slight noise and realized Sally had come back into the apartment and was outside the door.

"Am I interrupting you?"

Sara turned, bare-breasted and said, "No, actually you can help by stringing this wire over my shoulder to the sending unit clipped to my waistline in the rear."

Sally stared at her for a second and Sara turned so she could help with the wire. She did and Sara turned back around and slipped the cami on, adjusted the mic and put her cami and blouse back on and began buttoning it.

"I was so upset last night, I hardly looked at you. You were a cop with horrible news. But, now, your hair down and makeup on and without your...well, you know...you are so beautiful."

"Why, thank you! That's such a sweet thing to say. I really appreciate it."

Sally turned pink, then turned around.

"Sally, would you check with the detectives on the patio to see if they are ready for a system check for me? Thanks, dear!"

The young woman came back shortly and said the system was up. Sara spoke in normal tones, her head held as if she were speaking to someone in the room and said, "Testing. This is a test, test, test."

Cindy walked in a minute later, "Sounds good, Bob says. We are ready if blondie shows up." Sara looked down at the old Rolex she had put on today. She usually wore something tough and much less valuable, like the SEAL watch she did water sports in, but today she wanted to look the part she was playing. They had a half hour.

The three women went out to the patio and met with Bob.

"How about 'control' as the panic word, used like 'control yourself?'"

"Sounds good to me, Sara. What are you packing?" Bob asked.

"Backup gun in an ankle holster."

"Cindy?"

"My issue 9mm in my big purse, which I will stay very close to."

"Okay. I have my issue pistol plus an M-4 carbine in 5.56 in case things go 'way south."

"So, I guess we are ready. Now, as Churchill said, "they also serve who stand and wait." Sara said.

"Where do you get this stuff?" said Bob.

"I read a lot."

"Look at you. Learned and you aren't even half bad looking. You need to get a life."

Sara reached over and lightly pinched his cheek and did a Sandra Bullock imitation from Miss Congeniality, "Oh, you looove me!"

Bob jumped back and said, "Now, behave!"

To which Sara responded, "You love it. You know you do. You are such a pig! That's why I love you."

******

Allie had considered this dinner a real risk, but was somewhat turned on by the danger. But, she was careful. While the detectives were, unknown to her, teasing one another with the comradery that characterized their division, she was driving a surveillance detection route, or SDR, around the neighborhood well before time for her to arrive for dinner. She had not been trained by a member of the US Intelligence Community about SDRs; she did not know what one was. But, she did know that what she was doing was a prudent way to reduce risks.

This time of year, it was still light enough for her to wear her sunglasses. With them, a temporary baseball cap, and the Florida maximum tint on her Altima's windows, she could have been male or female and was largely unseen behind the glass.

Within two blocks, she saw four possible police vehicles. One was a marked unit from a nearby city. Out of his jurisdiction, so definitely was cop who lived here. One could go either way. It was a blue Tahoe, but the windows were dark. The third was an Impala that was down from the apartment as she cruised by. She felt that one was a hit. The last was a Florida Highway Patrol cruiser. It was at the outer extremity of the search area. She was not going to fight that. Too much law enforcement presence. She turned and headed due east to I-75. In an hour, she could be at a lesbian bar in Naples and find a less chancy and more suitable person.

Once on I-75 Southbound, Allie took off the baseball cap. She was wearing a flowery sundress that was backless and did not have much more material on the front. Other than some matching medium height sandals, she was not wearing anything else. She got off the first Naples exit and pulled into the lot of a club she knew. "The game's afoot, Watson!" she thought to herself as she turned on the visor mirror and checked her makeup. "Yep. I'd do me!" she thought. And, she would. As a matter of fact, that is exactly who has been "doing her" for some time.

At the apartment, Sally and the three detectives waited, still all in character. By nine, they decided to call it a night. Bob packed his gear, gave Cindy a ride to her car and they left.

"Sally, if she comes later, don't answer the door. Keep the lights out after I leave, okay?"

"Do you think I'm in danger?"

"Not really. I'm just being careful. What arrangements have been made for Alana? Murderers sometimes go to funerals of their victims. Where will she be buried? Hagerstown?"

Sally filled up again. "No, here actually. Her parents have a condo in Cape Coral and plan to both retire here soon and be buried here. They just didn't know they would have to bury their daughter first. But, the funeral will be in several days, at the First Methodist here in town. At eleven a.m."

"Thanks, I will be there, but generally out of sight watching for someone on the periphery. So, if you see me, please don't acknowledge it."

"That will be hard to do, Sara. I seem drawn to you as a symbol of strength and safety."

Sara reddened a tiny bit at this and acknowledged by saying that it was her job to be such.

She reached out and took Sally's hands in hers.

"I truly am sorry for your loss. You deserved better in life. You are bright and lovely."

Sally sobbed and reached over and hugged the detective, who after a second held her tightly as she cried. A few moments passed and Sally reached up and found Sara's lips and kissed her lightly. Sara did not pull away but kissed her back for several seconds.

"You should get some rest. Are you off work through the funeral?"

"I couldn't get off. My small-minded small business employer does not recognize non-traditional relationships, so there was not time. I have used all my vacation time except for the funeral."

"I will wait here and you go get ready for bed. When you are safely tucked in, I will let myself out. Can I do the deadbolt as I leave?"

"No, but I will get ready and let you out, if—you have to leave."

"I do. So, get ready, okay?"

"Come with me?"

"'Way too tempting. For now...'"

"How about stand near the door so we can talk, like when I helped you with the wire—which you still have on!"

"Oh, shit! You are right! I turned it off but didn't take it off."

She unbuttoned her blouse and slipped the cami over her head. Sally sat looking at her appreciatively and helped with the wire harness, brushing her hand unabashedly against a beautiful, hardened pink nipple. Sara quickly put the cami on, then the blouse.

"I feel so guilty about how you are affecting me right now, Sara. I mean my significant other was just murdered.

Maybe it's because we traded around and did a little swing-ing…did you ever do that?"

"No. Just one person at a time."

"Maybe you should try…"

"No, I don't think so. But, that doesn't mean I don't think you are really one great person. You have it all. But, you are worried about guilt. I am worried about profession-alism. I should not, and never have mixed business with pleasure. You are both, Sally. So, everything has to stay at that level. Okay?"

Sally went into the bedroom and returned wearing a silk robe. She walked Sara to the door.

As Sara got ready to open the door, Sally said "this is for the 'Later? Who knows? part'" and dropped the robe to the floor, standing there naked.

She was a natural 36D, with a tiny waist and flat stom-ach. Her legs were toned and tan. She pirouetted and Sara saw a bottom like a heart upside down and a shapely back, that complemented a perfect front.

With the pretty face and shining hair, she was anyone's dream of the ideal girl next door.

Sara drank the view in and slowly let out the breath she was holding.

"Oh, honey. I really have to go now. You really are superb!"

She turned and left while she could. Though she was beat, this would be a great night for candles around the bathroom and a long, hot bath.

CHAPTER 6

Like Allie, Leticia Foreman drove south to get to a club and maybe hook up with someone tonight. She was a successful mortgage broker who operated in the southern most extreme of Osprey County. The tall auburn-haired beauty was well-liked and well-respected in the local real estate community. She had a waterfront home on a canal and a twenty-five-foot center console from which she and some girlfriends fished local tournaments. Most neighbors and associates attributed her lack of a known man in her life to her being busy and fiercely independent—a modern woman who did not hesitate to fish twenty miles off shore for grouper and put her boat back in the slip at the marina at three in the morning. In fact, most people were envious of her carefully laid out, fun life.

Leticia did not make any effort to hide her sexual preferences. She was generally conservative in her personal life and exuded femininity and it simply did not come up very often. Having a boat and being able to go out of direct view of houses and beaches was very convenient. But, sometimes, like tonight, she just got an itch for some adventure. So, off she went to a classy lesbian club in the classy city of Naples.

She thought while driving; sometimes, driving was cathartic for her. Tonight, she was busily organizing her goals. Business goals were not among them. She was doing just fine, thank you.

She had fought weight all of her life and, being tall and very pretty, had often camouflaged the odd bulge with careful choice of clothes. While she was nowhere near her all-time high, she knew that, as she progressed into her forties, losing would become increasingly difficult.

So, she had recently gone on a doctor-supervised weight loss program and, also under her doctor's supervision, an exercise regimen. Leticia knew that many people boasted about hitting a "high" exercising. She had never accomplished that. She, instead, hit a "tired." But, she was going to try. And, when Leticia Foreman set out on a track, she always stayed on it. Before, she had just dabbled (and nibbled) at fad diets, diet shakes and gyms where everyone else had a beautiful body. No more. Her structure would not healthily support a size six, but she sure as hell was not going to spend another year as a size fourteen. At the next tournament weigh-in, she was going to be in a bikini and not covering up a tank suit with an over-sized tee-shirt.

******

The CSI team with the supermarket video tape scanned it for hours. Then, Maura did. They collectively found the victim walking to her car and a tall person getting in with her. Nothing usable, except the time stamp for the frames tallied with the TOD. They enlarged the view of the tall person but got nothing but an estimate of height. It was not even possible to tell the person's gender.

Maura had entered the information she needed on VICAP. Following a hit from VICAP, Maura placed a call to the Georgia Bureau of Investigation or GBI. She had worked with them before and considered them, the Texas Rangers and Florida's FDLE among the best state investigative agencies extant.

She found that the agent who had worked the multiple female throat-cutting case had just retired. He had worked the Thomasville, Georgia area and had retired there, according to the analyst to "decimate the population of Gentlemen Bobs in South Georgia." Maura had no idea what on earth that meant.

She knew she may well be on to something, but decided not to text or call Sara until she had something concrete. Maura was not given the direct number of the agent, but was told that the analyst would have him call her. He did at eight that night. And, what he had for her was golden.

He authorized his former analyst to send the case file to her at the Sheriff's Office. It would arrive the next morning. Upon learning this, Maura sent Sara a text that laconically stated "Have similar case from South Georgia. File coming tomorrow AM. Looks promising."

Sara read it in the car on the way home. Notwithstanding billboards about texting, Florida law allows law enforcement officers to use texts while driving. It is almost a necessity.

She arrived at her house and fed and played with Gibbs and DiNozzo. Sara then called Lynn and brought her up to date. She did what she did too often; she skipped dinner instead of eating just before sleeping. She did draw a steaming bath and put her favorite essential oils in it. She lit candles and stepped in. With an audible "Ahhh..." she laid her head back on a pillow on the rear of the garden tub and closed her eyes. She thought about the case. She thought about life. Then, she thought about Sally standing there at the door as she was leaving tonight. Leaving had been the smart thing to do. The right thing. But, having done the right thing, she decided to think about that vision a long time. So, she did.

The next morning, she was awakened at six by DiNozzo standing on her chest staring intently at her. What actually awakened her was his sandpaper tongue brushing against the tip of her nose. Not yet knowing the kittens when she had gotten them, she had misnamed them. DiNozzo was the clear leader and Gibbs the subordinate. But, it was too late to change their names, so she kept that as her little secret.

She hit the shower and put on 511 khakis, a thin Kevlar vest, her Sheriff's golf shirt and gear. She swung around back upon arriving at the office and topped of Argo's tank at the police pumps.

As she walked in, Maura called out and she went over to her cubicle.

"Sara, medium news first. We have the Morton woman on the supermarket tape pushing her basket to her car. Then, she speaks with another person. We cannot get any solid description of the second person, but we have a great timeline from the time stamp on the video. They talk for about three minutes; they get in the car and about five minutes later, that person gets out and walks out of sight of the camera. I had the CSIs cull out the part with the vic and perp and convert it to its own short video. It was emailed to you about time you walked in."

"Good! I felt my phone buzz a minute ago," Sara said.

"The bigger thing is that while the case file has not gotten in yet, but we may have something. A madam in Thomasville, Georgia area was murdered ten years ago. She was known to carry a pearl-handled straight razor. It and some money were missing. Then, four females turned up dead from having their throats slit about seventy-five miles away. Then it all stopped."

"Damn! Any suspects?"

"Not really."

"Were the victims' lesbians?"

"Unknown."

"I wonder if the perp just went to some other location

and kept it up and that department—or those departments—just didn't report the similar crimes to VICAP?"

"Sara, I was thinking the same thing. That system could be so valuable if we'd just feed it!"

"Okay, Maura. I have to do surveillance at Alana Hixon's funeral tomorrow. Assuming I can talk the LT into it, I may take a run up to Georgia and talk to the agent face to face. That will give me time to get back and be at the funeral."

"Want some help watching there? I am hidden in plain sight."

"That would be great! It will be a big help to me, and would get you out of the office. Do you need to clear it with LT?"

"Why don't you mention it when you go in to see him about going to Georgia?"

"I will. I'll let you know."

Sara went back to her cubicle and returned some phone calls and emails. She got a fresh cup of coffee and walked down to the Lieutenant's office.

"Got a second?"

"Enter!"

"Morning, Boss. Last night was a bust. She did not show."

"Why do you think that was?"

"Could be two things. She saw the murder on the news and didn't either want to get involved or figured she would be intruding at a bad time. Or, she's the murderer and wasn't going to come anyway."

"Which one do you think it was, Sara?"

"The first. Listen, I have two requests for you, both logical and reasonable."

"Oh-oh. A sales job. Go ahead."

"We may have a break in the case. Maura went into VICAP and found a similar case in Thomasville, Georgia. Five women. All had their throats slit. Then, it stopped.

The GBI agent just retired, but has shared the case file and is willing to talk to me and let me poke around."

"How long ago?"

"Ten years. I figure he went somewhere else and kept on and it just was not connected and reported like it should have been."

"Logical. So, you want to go to Thomasville. That's not too bad. Just north of Tallahassee. What, less than a day's drive or a quick flight and a rental car?"

"Yessir. I can do it in one day."

"A friend of mine is chief deputy with a department by Tallahassee. It's the closest airport to Thomasville, Georgia, I think. Let me see if he has a spare car he can lend you. That way, you will have a radio and the ability to run, if you need to. So, what's the other thing?"

"My second vic's funeral is tomorrow. I want to do surveillance in case the killer shows up in the periphery. Maura wants to be, as she says, "hidden in plain sight." I'd really appreciate the help."

"If she's willing, I'm willing. Need Bob or Cindy?"

"I don't think so. This sounds like it will be pretty small and private. Too many cop-looking people will spook him if he shows. Thanks, Boss."

"Just get this thing solved. The County Commissioners are reading about a serial killer and watching it on the news, and are all over Rob Roy's ass. They are afraid it will hurt tourism."

"And, concerned about the lesbian population being killed off?"

"Yeah, right. They are concerned about dollars. That's it."

She nodded and got up and left, happy that she had gotten both requests approved. She went by Mary Higgins's desk and requested that she try to get a quick round trip flight to the state capitol for her, returning as late as possible today.

Mary brought her an E-ticket. The LT called to say that his buddy would have a loaner sedan waiting for her at Tallahassee Airport. Sara had already told Maura to dress for a funeral tomorrow.

She pushed the Charger hard to get to the airport in time. The most direct flight at the time she needed was at the Sarasota Airport, an hour and a half north.

She made it in time, but had not provided sufficient notice for a local officer to fly armed, so she locked her pistol in the trunk of her sedan and flew as a civilian.

The flight was short and she met a deputy from Jim Gonzalez' friend's agency at the greeting area. He gave her the keys to a brown Crown Vic and told her how to drop it off for them that evening at the airport. She thanked him and got instructions on how to get onto Rt. 319, circle the city and go straight to Thomasville. She had the retired agent's address plugged into her phone and would let the GPS-map lead her to his house. She stopped on the way and got lunch at a local barbecue.

Former GBI special agent George Abernathy lived five miles outside of town. She was able to navigate directly to his house, which she found was actually a small farm.

He greeted her from the covered porch as she pulled into the yard. He was a fairly short man, stocky on first glance, powerful upon a second, longer look. He appeared to be about sixty.

"You must be Sara! Call me George."

She shook hands and admired his strong, but not over-powering grip. Here was a man who had no need to prove himself to anyone and she liked him immediately.

They sat on the porch. There was a pitcher of sweet tea on the small, round table between the chairs and a couple of glasses. He poured her one and she remembered how much she used to like real sugar, before switching over to healthier stevia.

"So, George, here's what I have going on down on the West Coast of Florida…" and she fully filled him in on the two murders.

"Well, if it's the same guy, and the MO is real close, you are going to have a couple more before you either catch him or, like with me, he just moves on. The women all more or less looked alike. The newspaper called them plump blondes. I thought they were strawberry blondes built like a woman should be, personally. Each one had her throat cut. All were naked, but the medical examiner did not find signs of sex before the attack…or, after, as far as that goes. There were no signs of defensive wounds. These women must have known or trusted the killer. I gave a lot of thought to the killer being in some sort of uniform. Maybe even a cop. Particularly since he never left even a smidgen of evidence behind."

"George," Sara asked, "were any or all of the four victims lesbians?"

"I don't rightly know. Ten years ago in this rural county, anybody with a different persuasion didn't advertise it. They could have been, but I don't have any reason to believe one way or the other."

"Were they married or single?"

"All were late twenties, early thirties and three were unmarried."

"George, are you aware of any lesbian clubs or bars in the area?"

He chuckled and she looked at him quizzically.

"I was just thinking, before that Rudolph guy blew up the lesbian and gay club in Sandy Springs in '97, we just kinda thought of bars as bars and didn't segregate them as to clientele. I guess we have to now. Seems like a step backwards to me."

Sara smiled and said, "Does to me, too, George."

"But, to answer your question: no, not specifically. The place where the first victim worked as a madam is still operating. They claim to just be a club now, catering to 'open-minded men and women.' They are still a brothel. I chased after them for a while, but could not get the powers that be locally, especially the sheriff in those days, to support me much."

"Sounds like 'Best Little Whorehouse in Georgia!"

George broke out in a hearty laughter that lasted a minute before he spoke again.

"I loved that movie. Even took the Missus to Atlanta to see the Broadway play version. Yes, Miss Rose Douglas was as pretty as Dolly, even in her late forties. The sheriff, now, he was no Burt. Not by a long mile, Sara. But, he had power and the ability to look the other way. It's not that the current sheriff is that way—he's not. He's a fine lawman. It's just that this rural area has a lot more pressing problems like meth labs, homegrown terrorists on both ends of the spectrum and the like. One half-ass brothel just doesn't rank high in anybody's 'to do' list."

"I guess I can see that, George. Tell me, is anybody who was there then, still there?"

"Yes. Though she would never admit to it, the 'social director' of the club was an 'entertainer' when Rose was killed and the others followed. The rest of the girls—and a coupla boys—are typical bordello types, they moved on."

"Do you think you could arrange for me to go over there and talk to her? Maybe as a woman, I could get something out of her that is would be more difficult for a man to do.

"She considers me an enemy. It would be better if I gave you directions and you went without me. Her name is Louisa Love, or at least that's the one she uses professionally. About your age, and pretty. I almost think she and Rose had a thing going with each other. That may help. I don't see a gun. You carrying?"

"No, as you know unless you are any kind of fed, you have to have a reason to be armed on board if you are just a nobody state or local and have to also send an NLETS message a day before, and so forth. The rule sucks. We are real cops; half the feds I know—and I was an NCIS special agent for years—never drew a gun on anybody. Pisses me off."

"Always did me, too. Wait a minute."

George disappeared into the house and returned with a small revolver with a short barrel.

"Your flight late enough that you'll have time to return this?"

"It is. Thanks, George. I really appreciate that. I will have it back to you this afternoon, hopefully unfired."

"I doubt you will need it at the Junction Social Club. What worried me was that you are driving an obvious police car and carry yourself like a cop. When I was with Atlanta PD and we responded on a bar fight, nobody would come at us. What I found out when I got out here in the boondocks is that the deputy is often attacked as soon as he walks through the door. Dumbass rednecks seem to think it's a sign of their masculinity to take on a cop, even if they lose. Which they usually do. I just don't want to have some idiot try to impress the boys by taking you on and you not having anything but your fists to back you up."

He gave her directions for the ten-minute drive and Sara fired up the old Crown Vic.

She turned off the county road onto a winding lane that led to a Victorian-era two story house. It was quite attractive. She parked the car and walked up the two steps onto the wide porch and knocked on the door. A very pretty young black woman answered, looked at her and the car and immediately knew Sara's profession. Just as she knew the profession of the woman with a fancy hairdo, full makeup and a negligee on.

"Help you officer?"

"Yes, Ma'am. I need to speak very briefly with Ms. Love."

"May I inquire about what?"

"You may. I am a Florida deputy. I am investigating a series of murders that may be related to the murder of Ms. Rose Douglas. She may know something that will help me stop them and put the person who killed Ms. Douglas behind bars…or, under order for lethal injection."

"Wait a minute. I'll see if she's in."

"Yeah, right!" Sara thought to herself, but just nodded and smiled pleasantly.

About two minutes later, the door opened again and an attractive late thirties brunette, with whose breasts were disproportionately larger than the rest of her petite frame, was visible through the crack in the door.

"What can I do for you, officer?"

"I am Detective Sara Nichols, from Osprey County, Florida. I have several murders I'm investigating that seem to tie back to the murder of Ms. Rose Douglas and four others here. I have no jurisdiction whatsoever in Georgia and no interest in the Social Club. I just want to put a killer behind bars, and I bet you'd like it too, if I did."

"Okay. You can come in for a minute." She turned to the first woman and said, "Keep things quiet so the detective and I can talk in my office without interruption." Sara knew that meant to advise everyone there that there was a cop in the house. She did not see any customer vehicles, but suspected there was a rear parking lot that was out of sight of cops and pissed off wives.

As they walked through the main hall and past the parlor, Sara realized why she did not like Victorian décor. Louisa, or perhaps Rose before her, was the Queen of

Uncomfortable Chairs. She hoped the rooms had more comfortable beds, though doubted that the patrons would know the difference.

Louisa Love's office was also Victorian, but the electronics were not. She had a top-grade Apple computer system and screens (which she immediately darkened) that watched rooms, the parking lot in front and the suspected one in back, which did have cars in it. Some were likely employees, most probably not.)

"So. You have gotten this far without a warrant. Prove you are not really a fed or the IRS."

Sara passed her badge case with ID over to her. She scrutinized it closely before returning.

"Sure you are not a task force officer assigned to the feds?"

"I am sure. I was NCIS before a deputy. I have had enough of the feds. Ms. Love, I don't give a shit about what type of business you have here. I just want to catch a killer. And, when I do, I suspect he will be the one that killed your predecessor."

"I'll open up to you if you will to me. Deal?"

"That depends. What do you want me to open up about?"

"Okay. I'm bi. My gaydar says you are either bi or a lesbian. Well?"

"Yes."

"Thank you for that. A little truth goes a long way. Rose and I were more than business associates. We had a relationship. You can understand that."

"Yes. I can both understand it and sympathize with you."

"Even in my line of work?"

"Look, Louisa—can I call you that? —human beings are human beings. They have needs. Your profession has been around a long time. There are those who would even argue it's a victimless crime. Some things in life were made illegal by legislators' ideas of morality, religion or the pressure of moneyed interests. I enforce the law in Florida. That does not mean I always agree with each law, just like I don't hate the people I arrest, unless they are real scumbags.

"What do you want to know?"

"Who do you think killed Rose Douglas?"

"That weird-ass stepson, Allen Douglas."

"Why?"

"Rose was a good businesswoman and a great lover. But, she had her issues. She figured since he was not her kid, she could have her way with him from about age thirteen until he left in his early twenties."

"Did she physically abuse him ever?"

"Maybe when he was younger and didn't want to cooperate."

Sara read "maybe" as "yes."

"Did he ever work here as an escort or entertainer, or whatever term you use?"

"Yes. He was tall, but slim and kinda pretty. Some of the gay guys always requested him, real pervs did when he was young, like early teens, and some of the horny nervous housewives didn't find him as intimidating as a bigger man."

"Sounds like you were a real full-service operation."

"Like I said, Rose was a good businesswoman."

"Where is Allen Douglas now?"

"Dunno. He left shortly after Rose was killed. He took all the cash on hand with him. Nobody ever saw or heard from him again. Nobody missed him, the mind-game playing manipulative bastard."

"Didn't that make him the automatic suspect?"

"Not when he was the sheriff's nephew."

Sara, writing in her notebook, looked up. "So, Rose was married to the sheriff's brother?"

"Yep."

"Was she doing both at the same time?"

"No, never. Everybody thought so, because he spent a lot of time here and kinda looked out after us. But, he did it because of his brother, who really cared for Rose, but died when the kid was about twelve. He had married her just after his wife died. The Sheriff was actually doing one of our girls and married her after divorcing his wife. Took to taking too many erectile dysfunction pills and had the big one in the saddle about five years ago. Left my girl pretty well off. Of course, we are on our own now, so to speak."

"So even the GBI, which looked into the serial killer thing, did not like this Allen character for the murder or murders?"

"Well, the sheriff kinda made sure that nobody talked about him or his abrupt departure from the scene. So, they didn't know about him to suspect him. Just after Rose was killed and the rest of the murders started, election time came around. His closeness to us finally pissed off the churchgoers and he didn't get re-elected after being the sheriff for twenty years. I think it was kind of a relief to him. But, his last act was to cover his nephew by his brother's first wife."

"Was Allen gay?"

"Don't know what his real preferences were. All of us are actors in a way. He was with men, when Rose made him, women, when she made him and her, when she made him. Before you judge her too hard, he was already having sex with girls by the time she married his father. It's not like she was doing a kid she raised from a toddler or something."

"I'm not here to pass judgment, Louisa, just to solve a crime. You said he was tall, slim and kind of pretty—can you give me a more detailed description?"

"He might have changed. I have not seen him for ten years. Then, he was maybe five eleven, a hundred forty pounds, light brown hair and green eyes. He looked for the world like he should have been gay, but I always sensed he wasn't."

"Why?"

"I can't really put my finger on it. Just a gut thing."

"Were you ever with him?"

"Hell, no! He was Rose's and so was I. Would not have been either right or safe."

"I heard she had a pearl-handled straight razor. Was it in the inventory of her possessions when she died?"

"That and about five thousand in cash were taken. But, it wasn't a robbery. No sign. No struggle, and she was killed in her bed at night. Never put up a fight."

Sara did not elaborate, but she had read the case file on the short flight up and neither had the four others put up a fight.

"What do you know about the other four victims? Were they lesbians? Ever customers here?"

"No, none were 'out' while they were here. This is a small community. Rose would find runaway girls at the bus station or hitchhiking and get them off the streets. She felt like that at least here, they would have a place to sleep, good food, no drugs and no brutal pimps to beat them and rape them. When they were ready, she gave them some money, legally had their names changed through the sheriff and his judge friend, gave them some money and relocated them. She may have been tough to the world, but she had a heart. From a bad picture in the paper, I think one of the four was a girl from here. I heard from Rose that she got married to a guy who used to know her here, but had moved away. Rose thought he beat her, so that's why she left him. He still dropped by though, since he liked the club and had family in the area.

"Could her ex-husband have found out and somehow blamed Rose, then killed the others as a subterfuge for then killing his wife?"

Louisa Love started laughing. Sara looked at her with a puzzled look.

"That asshole spent every spare dollar he had here screwing his brains out before they moved away and some after. Rose kinda liked him. He tended to like black girls; I always thought it was because Rose looked too much like his wife in the dark! So, no, I don't think he was the killer. As a matter of fact, I know it. He was in jail for DUI when Rose was killed. He had screwed away his potential bail money and had to sit it out behind bars. Jerk!"

"So, we are back to the step-son?"

"Yeah, but maybe it's because I just did not like him. Rose did in a weird sort of way. I never saw them pass a cross word or look."

"Interesting! They got along?"

"They did."

"Louisa, did Allen sleep with any of the other girls that were here then...or boys?"

"Pretty sure he didn't. Rose had an ironclad rule about not crapping where you eat. Except for her and me"

"Are any of the girls who were here when this all happened still here?"

"No."

"Is there anything else you can think of that might help me catch this guy, whoever he is?"

"Naw, I've told you everything I know."

"Well, you have been a big help and I really appreciate it. I may try to get a sketch artist to come by and let you describe this Allen guy for a picture, since he seems to be my top suspect. Will you do that?"

"Maybe...maybe not."

"Okay. I will call you when I get this guy, okay?"

They exchanged business cards and Sara left for George's house, shared what she had learned and returned his gun and went to the airport. She turned the county car in and boarded her flight for Sarasota.

She did not do a lot of thinking on the plane, except for George's distaste at having been engineered out of the picture on Allen Douglas. He agreed that Douglas was now a suspect.

Sara did think of one other killing in history that had a slight similarity. Always a fan of Western history, she knew that the woman outlaw, Belle Starr, was killed by shotgun blast in 1896.

The primary suspect, Ed Watson, had fled to Florida, where he was dastardly enough that many of the citizens of the town of Chokoloskee joined to summarily gun him down as he approached Smallwood's General Store to buy groceries. However, others at the time thought the real killer of Belle Starr was none other than her son, Ed Reed, who she had beaten savagely for mistreating her famous black horse. Maybe Allen Douglas was her Ed Reed…

CHAPTER 7

Sara got in late and fixed a simple salad for dinner, after seeing to Gibbs and DiNozzo. She sat by her pool in nothing but a long tee-shirt and sipped a cup of green tea with pomegranate.

First thing tomorrow, she would put Maura on tracking down Allen Douglas, based on the sketchy information she had as to name, approximate age, town of birth. The latter might be more beneficial than using law enforcement resources, as she could go online to the Georgia Vital Records and get a lot from his birth certificate to supplement searches of law enforcement and other data bases, such as Google. A parallel search could be for the late sheriff, giving his brother's particulars to use for finding the son. It was just a matter of patiently connecting lines.

The next morning, Sara was sitting at her desk typing away on her computer on a case report with her findings from yesterday. She would have to leave early to go home and exchange the Charger for her Jeep to take to the funeral for surveillance. She wondered if the killer was really Allen Douglas, and if he would be there, and, even if he was, how could she recognize him?

She finished the report and her ideas about a search plan for Douglas and put one copy on Maura's desk and one on the LT's. Both had a note that she was leaving to prepare for the funeral at 0900. She did not know where Maura lived, so she was unaware whether the crime analyst would come in first or go straight to the funeral.

Maura did come in and was dressed formally for the funeral. Sara saw her pick up the report and begin to study it. She gave her fifteen minutes to absorb it before walking over with her second cup of tea.

"What do you think my story should be if I have to talk to the family?"

"The truth is always the simplest. I'd just tell them that you are part of several people there representing the Sheriff's Office and you are very sorry for their loss."

"Plausibly deniable?"

"And, true," Sara responded. "I have to run back home, drop off the official ride and pick up my Jeep. When you see me and ignore me, it will be in a subdued bright orange Jeep Wrangler with a hardtop. I will be wearing sunglasses and probably a big straw sun hat."

"'Subdued' bright orange. An oxymoron! So, you will be hiding is plain sight too?"

"I will be. I may get out or may not. I will have my handheld in a large purse to call for the cavalry in case we need it. But, I doubt that we will."

"Let's hope so! That would bring a conclusion to the case and the killings."

"If you look at it that way, you are right, I guess. Well, anyway, I will not 'see' you there!"

"Good! I look forward to not 'seeing' you also!"

Sara left and drove back to her house. She put on a black sundress and formal sandals. She picked a large matching bag and put her 9mm and badge, handcuffs and the handheld radio in it. She selected a black straw sun hat with a wide brim and sunglasses that had wide dark circular lenses and were far less cop-like than her usual mirrored aviators. She thought she looked quite sophisticated and very up-town, as she hefted the bag with the gun and handcuffs.

She called Sally and checked on her.

"Hey, it's Sara. How are you doing? Ready to go?"

"Ready as I will ever be. Are you going to be there?"

"Yes, but I will be watching for the blonde and maybe a guy, based on a lead I got yesterday. You have to pretend not to know me, so don't let your facial expression give it away, okay?"

"Will I see you later?"

"Maybe, but if so, only briefly. I have some leads to follow very quickly on both murders and need to see if they are connected to some in Georgia."

"It is a serial killer then?"

"I don't know for sure ours represent serial murder. The ones in Georgia certainly do. But, Sally. The press or TV people will find you. Don't give any interviews or statements. I don't want you exposed to the public for fear the killer will be watching. It would be very imprudent to talk to the media."

"Okay, if you say so. I should say I know who the killer is so he can come for me and you can kill him."

"Too dangerous. Let's file that one away for a last resort."

"If you are in disguise, how will I recognize you?"

"Remember, you will not recognize me or acknowledge me in any way. I am in a black dress, black wide-brimmed hat and driving an orange Jeep. I probably will not be at the church service, only the graveside rites. That's where the killer is most likely to turn up."

"I bet you look hot!"

"One thing is for sure, we will all be hot in the Florida sun that time of day at the graveside rites! I have to run. I will see you there."

"Can't wait!"

******

At nine-thirty in the morning, the Audi mechanics were putting a two-year old A6 on the lift. The driver's side front tire had struck an object sharp enough to totally deflate it in less than a second. Luckily, the driver, who was going a bit too fast on I-75 South, was adept and kept the shiny side up, as the car careened on its bare metal wheel. That wheel was virtually destroyed as were the driver's plans for the evening.

The driver, due in shortly to meet an insurance adjuster at the Audi dealership, was Leticia Foreman. She loved her red Audi and was miffed at herself for not seeing whatever it was on the road that had shredded her tire and almost sent her into the woods alongside the Interstate.

The incident had prevented her from going to her club in Naples and maybe hooking-up with someone interesting. But, maybe later in the week, what was left of it. Maybe the weekend, though Southwest Florida was a retirement haven, albeit a wealthy one. Unfortunately for her, she considered that the retirement aspect reflected in the age the lesbian population visiting clubs, especially on weekends.

Allie was drawn to the funeral; it would give her some sort of closure to the last cleansing, she thought. It would be too risky to go to the church part, but she had read in the obituary that there would be a graveside rite also. She would cruise that and see what the situation was. While she tried to avoid stupid risks, taking small ones was exciting to her.

She went to the cemetery fifteen minutes after the church portion was scheduled. She did not know how long the funeral would last. The fact that it was a Methodist church did not give her any guidance. She suspected that a Baptist or Catholic one might be longer but had no basis for estimation.

The cemetery was not that pretty, she thought. It was flat and tree-less and would be as hot as hell in an hour or whenever the people arrived at one of the two plots with the hole and the tent shelter. There was already someone waiting at one location. It was a woman in an orange Jeep. So, Allie slipped her sedan into the lane across the way where the other burial seemed to be anticipated. Since there were no name signs, she would have to wing it as to which one was Morton. She had gotten cheated on the Hixon funeral, since she did not find out until too late it was out of town.

Sara watched as the sedan pulled up to the funeral site across the lane. She waited and the person did not get out of the car. Knowing by vehicle and the way she looked and carried herself today, a vision of her would not scream "cop," she decided to perhaps prompt the person to take some sort of action. Like getting out of the car.

She climbed out of the Jeep. There was no wind to cool, even wearing a gauzy dress did not help. She walked over to the canvas roofed structure, not to choose a seat since they were for family, but to find a modicum of shade. Sara made a point of not looking back at the sedan across the lane. She took out a compact and pretended to put on fresh lipstick. She watched as the other person got out and did what she did, she walked to the tent and stood in the shade under it. The image in the small mirror was of a tall woman with thick black hair. She was not heavy, but she did not look like the description of the blonde POI. The legs she saw in the dress and the breasts convinced her this was not Allen Douglas in drag. Probably just an early arrival to the other funeral trying to find some shade.

Allie, sweating profusely from the heavy wig, looked around. Not a soul in sight. Shame the pretty bitch across the way was thin and had dark brown hair. Otherwise, she might have let her satisfy some of the anger she had suffered for years. But, a thin brunette…she had not gotten that bad off…yet. And, she was not on the list. She had to follow her plan. It was hot as hell. But, she had been in hotter places. No, cops or not, she decided to find fun elsewhere and got back in her car and left. As she drove past the hot brunette in black, she waved. The brunette waved and memorized her tag number.

After the sedan had left, Sara walked back to the Jeep and retrieved the handheld radio. She called in the tag number. It came back to a leased car to one Elizabeth Smith. Sara wrote down the information and Smith's address and continued to watch.

At the funeral, Maura scanned the crowd. She had rolled up the aisle to the casket. The parents were there and she gave her condolences. There was no mention on their part of relationship, whether it be from work or neighborhood, or school. Nobody seemed out of place and there were no blondes who met the description of the person of interest. It seemed like a bust unless the graveside rite ended up more productive.

She did not see the van parked in a lot across from the church. The man saw but did not pay any particular attention to her.

Maura went to her wheelchair-equipped van. It was already in the small procession lined up for the drive to the cemetery. An Osprey deputy in a marked unit led the procession the several miles. He was aware that a surveillance op was going on and was ready to divert and assist upon receiving a call from Sara. None came.

Sara, once she was sure the killer was not there, eased the Jeep by the grave. Only Sally and the parents and some aunts and uncles remained. Sally looked up and saw the lovely brunette driver, her sky-blue eyes hidden by big round sunglasses, drive by slowly. She did not acknowledge the

Jeep or its driver but smiled for the first time today.

Sara headed home to change and pick up the Charger for the rest of her workday. While en route, she entered the address on the sedan at the cemetery into her map app. It was worth checking out. The hair color was not right, but wigs and dye can change that very easily.

She changed, called in on the car radio and marked underway to that location. It was a medium-price apartment complex. The car was not there and there was no response to her knock on the door. That was not surprising since it was lunchtime during a workday. She found the rental office and went in.

She flashed her ID—the badge was obvious on her belt just in front of her gun—and asked for a workplace for the resident in apartment 3011.

"Joanie isn't there anymore. We were friends. It was heartbreaking. She was in an accident with a friend. The friend's car was T-boned and she was in the hospital with back problems. She got hooked on oxycodone. She lost her job and had to move out. I've tried to help her. Most of the time, she is at a half-way house in Cape Coral. I have the address if you need it."

"Thanks for that information. I do need it and will go straight there now."

"Is she in trouble?"

"Sounds like it! But, her oxy problems are unrelated to why I need to chat with her. It's about a case where she may be a witness."

"Good luck, detective. The drug has kind of addled her mind. She can't work in retail or as a server like she used to. I doubt if she can drive. It's really sad."

"You are right. Too many doctors prescribe and refill oxy from my perspective as a law enforcement officer. Thanks for your help. I will try to track her down."

Sara left and drove to Cape Coral and found the half-way house. The car was not there, but Joanie was. She was not the person at the cemetery, nor did she meet the description of the blonde POI.

"Joanie, I am Detective Sara Nichols. I would like to ask you a few questions. You are not in any trouble as far as I know. Will you help me?"

"Sure."

"First off, where is your car?"

"She has it."

"Who is 'she?'"

"You know!"

"No, I don't remember. Remind me," Sara said very conversationally.

"I used to be the hostess at the Oyster and Crab House."

"Yes. The car?"

"She gave me money for it and took it."

"Who did?"

"I don't know her name. She gave me three hundred dollars and took it."

"What does she look like?"

"Pretty."

"Was she tall? Thin? What was her hair color?"

"It was a Nissan."

"How old do you think she is?"

"I miss it."

Sara could tell she was not getting anywhere with the woman and probably no one would if and until she broke the cycle of prescription drug addiction. Her past experience with people hooked on oxy was you asked them one question and they looked you in the eye and answered another, totally unrelated question.

The only things she knew about the car was that it was in the general area and that the original leasee did not have it. She went to her car and checking her notes, found the name of the leasing company and called them. They were happy to hear from her, as there had not been a lease payment made for four months.

Sara advised them that the original leasee had been in a wreck in another vehicle and had lost operative control of the leased car. They should report it stolen, she recommended. She also noted Osprey County and that the Cape Coral area was where it had recently been spotted.

Not knowing when or if the leasing company would do that, she called Maura and gave the salient information to her to do a statewide be on lookout, or BOLO for the car. She knew agencies around Florida would have the car's license number and description in hand by the following day, at the very latest. Like so many cases, this one was likely to be solved by a traffic stop, one of the most dangerous things a police officer does in his or her day.

Back at the office, Sara called retired GBI agent Abernathy.

"Mrs. Abernathy, this is Detective Nichols from down in Florida. I met with George yesterday. Is he available?"

"No, he's doing his thing. Took the dogs and that old A.H. Fox shotgun and is out after Gentleman Bob."

"You know, I meant to ask him who Gentleman Bob was yesterday and forgot. Do you know?"

"Honey, it's not a 'who,' but a 'what.' Gentleman Bob is the bobwhite quail. Hunters in the South just say they are going 'bird hunting.' Everybody knows that while pheasants, doves, turkeys, ducks and all are technically birds, when you go 'bird hunting,' it's quail. It's a gentleman's sport and the bird is the Bob White, so...Gentleman Bob!"

"Thanks. I get it now! Would you have him call me when he gets in? He has my card with all my numbers."

"I will. Now, you be safe out there!"

"Yes Ma'am. I'll try. Thank you."

******

Sara got home around six o'clock and rummaged through the freezer after playing with and feeding Gibbs and DiNozzo. She found an ahi tuna steak and used the microwave to thaw it. Once done, she put some steamer bag peas and mushrooms in the microwave while she rubbed extra virgin olive oil on the tuna, then rolled it in sesame seeds. She put some EVOO in a pan and added garlic and capers. She sautéed the tuna and had it with the vegetables and two glasses of wine.

The phone rang. It was George returning her call.

"Hey, George! You having quail for dinner?"

"I sure am! Carolyn is frying up a mess of them right now! Wish you were here. Nothing finer!"

"I bet! When Louisa Love opened up and gave us a suspect that had been hidden from you during the original investigation, did that reopen the case? Because, if it did, I have a suggestion."

"I talked to my successor agent here. He was pretty darn interested in what you learned, so the answer is 'yes'."

"Does GBI use sketch artists? Do you know how valuable a sketch of Allen Douglas, maybe age-enhanced by a decade would be to him and to me?"

"We do, and real valuable! But, how are we going to get it?"

"I think I can work that through Louisa Love; I already mentioned it during the interview."

"She hates us."

"But, she also hates Allen Douglas. I think she will help us get him as long as a bunch of cops running around does not imperil her business operation."

"Well, like I said, one brothel is not a big deal anymore, especially if we could solve multiple cold murder cases and put a serial killer behind bars, maybe waiting for the injection."

"If you could get that agreed upon, I think I can sell Louisa to give the artist the description for the sketch."

"Tomorrow's Friday. I will get back to you no later than Monday afternoon, if not sooner."

"Thanks! Now go eat some 'birds.'"

"I will do just that. When you come up here next time, you will have to come by and have some—or, go out with the dogs and me and get your own."

"One way or the other, it's a deal, George. Thanks again. Have a great night!"

Sara ate the tuna and vegetables and took a third glass of wine out by the pool and sat in the dark. The screened cage or lanai protected her from the mosquitos. The two cats joined her and did what cats do best, curled up and went to sleep.

******

Leticia Foreman wanted to celebrate. She had had four mortgage closings this week. And, she had her Audi back and with a new wheel and tire. She knew she had been lucky by not having been hurt or worse when the tire deflated instantly on the Interstate.

She reprised her plan to go to the club in Naples. She found a royal blue sheath that showed her voluptuous figure off at its best, and some killer heels.

This time, she went to Naples without incident and parked at the club. She went in, hoping Thursday night would have an interesting crowd. It did. There were some really hot women in there. Nothing like money and Naples had plenty of it.

Leticia would make it a fairly short evening. She was taking half a day off on Friday to get the boat ready. There was a Captain's Meeting at Bonita Springs on Friday night and an Inshore Slam fishing tournament she and her three fishing partners had signed up for on Saturday. The slam for this tournament was snook, redfish, and sea trout.

She walked in and ordered a chocolate martini, calories notwithstanding. She would sweat it off in the boat tomorrow for sure.

A really good girl band was playing, and for once, Leticia thought, decent music. Kind of a Southern Rock, a girls' Lynyrd Skynyrd type thing. For some reason, too many of the clubs had to have some sort of dark, head-banging rock. This was nice and danceable. Leticia watched for a while and finished her drink and ordered another.

"Hi! Mind if I sit down?"

The person asking was her height, had long black hair and beautiful eyes with long lashes that looked real. She had a lot of cleavage showing and was wearing a simple black dress. All she was missing was a string of pearls.

"Sure! I'm Leticia. Sit down."

"Thanks. My name is Allie. It's my first time here, so I was sort of looking around for a friendly face. Yours looked friendly and beautiful, so I thought I would shoot for the moon right off the bat!"

"Aren't you sweet? Where are you from, Allie?"

"Oh, I'm just a Steel Magnolia from Dixie. See? I'm even drinking a mint julep."

"What are you doing in Naples?"

"Just looking around. I may relocate to here, so I'm getting the lay of the land. How about you?"

"I live about thirty miles up the Interstate. This is just about the classiest club on the West Coast of Florida, so I drive down every now and then."

"I'm certainly glad you picked tonight, Leticia!"

"Me, too! What is the talent that you are going to bring us here on the Sun Coast? You are tall enough to be a model..."

"But, I am hardly pretty enough to be a model! I am an accountant. That allows me to move around anywhere and still keep most of my clients."

"I'd argue the part about not being pretty enough to be a model. But, as a businesswoman, it surprises me that you can live anywhere and maintain tax accounting relationships. I would have thought you'd have to visit their homes and offices too much for that."

Allie's expression changed almost imperceptibly, but Leticia picked up on it. She said nothing. She was pretty sure she was being lied to and decided to just sit back and see where this thing went. Allie was pretty. But, why lie?

"Well. I am able to pull it off. Thank heavens. I am getting tired of North Florida. It's just like living in Georgia. Just different license plates."

"And, no state income tax," Leticia added to the accountant.

"Yes, of course. There is that. Would you like to dance?"

Since the conversation was not going that well, Leticia said," Sure."

The band was playing "Tuesday's Gone," and the two slow danced to the melancholy old classic.

They returned to the table to order more drinks at the end of the song.

"Wow, I am feeling woozy," Allie said. "My period must be starting. It always affects me that way. I need to go out to the car and get some tampons. Do you mind walking with me? The combination of music, alcohol and the period really has me unsteady."

"Of course, let me take you by the arm and help steady you."

"Thanks. This is embarrassing."

"Don't be silly."

"Which is your car?"

"I parked it towards the back, around the corner from the building."

Leticia was not feeling very positive about Allie or the whole situation. The little hairs on the back of her neck were starting to stick up.

They got to Allie's car and she opened the passenger door and leaned in. Leticia saw her emerge with some sort of shiny blade and with a wild look in her eyes from the headlights of a car now pulling into the parking lot.

Leticia swung her purse and caught Allie a glancing blow on the side of the head. It knocked off the long black wig, revealing lighter hair pulled back and pinned. Allie staggered back and recovered.

By this time, Leticia had kicked off her high heels and started to sprint for the front of the club.

Several women were getting out of the arriving Jaguar that had lit up Allie. Leticia yelled.

"Help me! There is a crazy woman with a knife! Somebody call the police!" She looked back and Allie was not running after her. She heard a car start and tires screech.

The dark sedan came flying around the building aiming for Leticia and the three women at the car by the front door of the club. One of the bouncers, a very solid woman with a short haircut, came out to see what the ruckus was about and saw Leticia dive over the trunk of the Jaguar as Allie's car glanced off the Jag and struck one of the women who was trying to get away.

Allie had her lights off and the lights in the parking lot were insufficient for the bouncer to get a full plate number. She had seen Leticia dive and the Nissan hit the other woman, so she dialed 911 and reported the incident, asking for a police and ambulance response.

The woman, who had been the driver of the Jaguar, was seriously injured. The club manager brought out several white tablecloths, one to try to place under her and one to make a pillow. Both actions were exactly wrong, well-intentioned or not. Leticia got up shakily. She had scrapes on both legs and her right shoulder was killing her where she had landed on it. But, she was alive. No thanks to the crazy bitch with the wig and the knife.

The Collier County 911 center had run the partial license and car description after passing the call to the Naples Police to respond and County Fire Rescue to respond.

The car hit on the BOLO Maura had put out four hours before and Collier County called Osprey County.

"We have a hit on that dark Nissan. A partial plate observed matches. It was involved in a female knife attack at a gay night club off Tamiami Trail in Naples. Thought you'd like to know."

"Do you have the subject and/or the vehicle?"

"Negative. It struck another person, probably sustained some damage and ran. We just alerted all our units and the Florida Highway Patrol. It was last seen going north on US 41."

"Thanks. I'll put some Osprey units at the county line on the Interstate and US 41 and alert our detective. She will probably want to respond. Do you have a detective unit assigned yet?"

"No, I just wanted to let you guys know early. I read this was about a multiple homicide. Looks like she was trying to add one tonight."

"Roger that. Will you give me a call back when you have a detective name?"

"Will do. Gotta catch another line now."

******

Sara's government cell rang beside her at the pool. She took the message but did not need to write down the address of the club. She knew it and had been there. It was a bit stuffy, but far enough out of her turf to make it one of her options.

She pulled on her usual outfit for work, said goodbye to Gibbs and DiNozzo and set the alarm as she went out the door towards the Charger.

"Come on, Argo. You get a chance to stretch your legs on the Interstate tonight!" She ran fast on the surface roads and hit I-75 South. She turned on the wig-wags and LEDs and accelerated up to triple digits and held it there all the way to the first Naples exit. Luckily, traffic was not heavy at this time of night. All the way, she kept lookout for the Nissan, but to no avail.

"4029?"

"4029 go!"

"4029, the detective assigned is Naples PD Detective Alfred Cruz. I have his number if you want it."

"I am running pretty hard right now; will you text it for when I get off Interstate?"

"10-4!"

"4029 out."

At the first Naples exit, she pulled off in the median and read the text. She tapped Cruz' phone number. He answered on the third ring.

"Detective Cruz."

"Hi, this is Detective Sara Nichols. I am working a double homicide that may be serial. Looks like you might have the first break in the case tonight with a live victim."

"Yeah. Seems so! What is your location?

"Just got off I-75 at first northern Naples exit."

"Damn! I just left the scene and am route to Naples Community Hospital. You must live in southern Osprey County. I can't believe you are here already!"

"Nope, live in mid-Osprey. I'll meet you in the hospital in a few."

"Copy that."

They hung up and Sara pulled onto the highway and headed for the hospital.

She saw a couple of NPD marked units and an obvious unmarked police car improperly parked in the ER lot. She improperly parked Argo beside the detective car and went in.

"Hi, where can I find all the other cops?"

"I'll take you. The victims are in two beds at the end of the hall."

As they were walking down the hall, Sara asked the ER nurse "What's their status?"

"We are stabilizing the car victim and prepping her for surgery. I don't have an official condition, but it's pretty grave."

Of the two curtained-off "rooms" at the end of the hall, one was totally closed off and seemed full of busy ER people. The other had three cops, two in police uniforms and one in a sports coat. That would be Alfredo Cruz.

"Detective Cruz? I'm Detective Sara Nichols."

He looked up and smiled. Literally looked up, since he was a handsome man about five-seven in height.

"Oh, hi. This is Ms. Leticia Foreman. We just got access to her for some questions, if you'd like to listen in."

"I would. Sounds like the person I have been looking for is who she encountered tonight."

The questions that followed were standard detective handbook. "What time did you arrive? Did you know the assailant? Why did she pick you? What did she look like? *Ad nauseum*.

"Detective, do you have anything you want to ask?"

"Yes, thanks. First, Ms. Foreman. I am working a double homicide one county north. It seems to be tied to five similar homicides in South Georgia ten years ago. You match the description of all seven victims as well as the weapon and type location. We have to catch this person and fast. You said the person was taller than you, maybe my height? Good! Thin and wearing a black wig over blonde hair? You said the person was buxom. Could you tell if they were real or a padded bra?"

"They were real. The outfit let a lot show."

"The person meets the description of a person of interest in my cases. Now, that person of interest has become a suspect. The previous suspect was a male of similar size. I have an artist's sketch of him, computer enhanced to add ten years coming in the morning. I'd like to show it to you."

"Sure. But this was definitely a woman. I slow danced with her."

Sara felt the disapproval from her fellow officers at this and frowned.

"Boy, this opens up a lot of possibilities. Two killers? One with a sex change? Wow," Sara thought out loud.

"Detective Cruz, any luck on the vehicle yet?"

"Not yet. And, we had the county and state on it within minutes. She must have found a garage or run it into a canal or something."

"Will you let me know when you find it?" He nodded yes.

"The description came from me. I saw the vehicle and maybe the suspect at the second victim's funeral yesterday."

"Why didn't you stop it?"

"We didn't know what kind of vehicle we were looking for. I was undercover in my personal Jeep Wrangler. The person was not acting suspicious and was actually at another graveside rite location nearby. Long shot."

"I'd have stopped it."

"Retrospectively, I should have called in some marked units. Just not enough to go on under that circumstances. Almost not enough for a BOLO; the person had thick black hair and got out and walked around the other grave in plain sight. Then, she waved at me as she drove by. Just looked like an early arrival for the funeral that followed. I just did the BOLO when I found out that the car had been given to an unidentified operator by the leasee, an oxy addict."

Cruz's expression showed he was not convinced her

procedures had been acceptable. Sara turned to the victim, Leticia Foreman.

"So, are they letting you out of here tonight?"

"Oh, yeah. I just have some scrapes and contusions from jumping over the Jag of the poor woman that got hit. I do suspect, detectives, that your suspect has a big blue bruise on the left side of her face where I whammed my heavy purse into it as hard as I could."

"Probably saved your life," Cruz observed. Sara thought that was at least one thing they could agree on.

"I have a team going out on my boat Saturday, for the fishing tournament starting tomorrow, so I need to get home and get some rest. I guess I can call a taxi."

"Where's your car?" Sara asked.

"At the club."

"I don't mind dropping you at the car. I have to get back up to Osprey County and it's just on the way. Okay with you, Detective? Once you are through here, of course."

"Yeah, that's okay. Ms. Foreman, here's my card. Call me if you think of anything you haven't told me that could be important, ya hear?"

"I will. I have to wait for the hospital to release me. Sure it's not an inconvenience, Detective Nichols?"

"No. I will confer with Detective Cruz for a minute and get some coffee. You want some?"

"You bet! Black, please."

"Coming up shortly." She walked out with the officers.

"I have to tell you; this puts a real wrinkle in my case. But, with the car and the knife, it must be related. A corrupt sheriff in Georgia hid the fact that the primary suspect up there was his nephew."

"Guess with this being a girl and all, that suspect is no longer a suspect," Cruz offered.

"Maybe still one up there. Involves a brothel. Every

victim, starting with the brothel madam—his stepmother who had sex with him—straight through to Leticia Foreman looked more or less alike."

"Were they all gay?"

"Maybe, maybe not; we don't know yet. Both in my jurisdiction were and Ms. Foreman is gay or she wouldn't have been where she was, dancing with the attacker."

"Think the guy in Georgia got converted to a girl?"

"Possible. By accounts, he was the right size and build to pull it off. Though the woman tonight and my blonde POI were reported as being very pretty. I guess there are impersonators and transsexuals who are beautiful, but… Funny thing is that the guy and the stepmother seemed to get along okay. But a pearl-handled straight razor was missing after he left and that seemed to match the weapon on every killing."

"A conundrum."

"It is. It sounds like the woman who was hit is pretty bad off. If that's a vehicular homicide, that would make eight murders with one suspect…at least that we know about. What we don't know is how many people this person has killed during the ten-year break."

"Gotta be related, Detective Nichols."

"Looks like we are going to be working together, so make it Sara."

"Okay, Sara. Call me Al."

"Easy to remember."

"Why? Your dad's name?"

"No. The POI uses the name Allie."

"Crap. That's right!"

"Here, Al. Let's swap cards. If I get anything more from Foreman tonight with girl talk in the car on the way back, I'll share it with you. Doubt if I do, she seemed pretty cooperative. But, sometimes people remember things."

"Thanks. We'll be talking, I'm sure, Sara. Have a good night."

"You, too."

Sara walked over to the snack shop. It was closed. She found coffee at a nurse's station and picked up two foam cups of black coffee and went back to the end of the ER. A nurse was in the process of releasing Leticia Foreman.

"Ready for a ride back to the club?"

"I'm ready for a ride to my car, then home to bed!"

"Let's do it."

When they got to the Charger, Sara tried the radio and it worked. It probably was bouncing off the southernmost Osprey County repeater tower.

"4029."

"4029 go."

"4029 is leaving Naples Community Hospital with one white female aboard. Mileage is 44,347."

"Copy one WF and mileage 44,347."

"Do you have to do that every time you have someone in your car, Detective?"

"It's Sara and yes, I do. It is really to protect you and to protect me from false accusations. Shame the world has gotten that way, but it has."

"Yes, unfortunately, it has. Please call me Leticia. Do you need directions back to the club?"

"No, I have been there a number of times."

"But, isn't it out of your jurisdiction?"

"Yes, but I am off work sometimes, too."

"I see."

"Tell me about the fishing tournament. My brother lives in Islamorada. I fish with him, his wife and kids every chance I get."

"It's an inshore grand slam. Technically, that's a flounder, redfish and sea trout. But, this is a Florida inshore grand slam, so a snook is substituted for the flounder."

"You gonna fish mangroves or beaches or bays like Pine Island Sound?"

"You do know your stuff! All, probably. Want to join our team sometime? I can't always get everyone together, so having a fourth would be great."

"That would be fine, depending on what cases I have going," she said, then asked

Leticia, is there anything else you can add that might help me catch this person?"

"Not really. She was gorgeous. Even with the wig. It was so expensive that I didn't know it was a wig until I knocked it off her head. She almost reminded me of some-one, more her mannerisms and the way the moved than her actual looks. Hmm…just don't know who, though. I couldn't help but overhear you and the other detective's conversation out in the hall. I really don't think she was a guy. Ever. She felt fit and strong, but had all the feminine curves and moved like a woman."

"This woman being the attacker literally ruins my case to date. I will try to get by and show you a likeness of the male suspect. Actually, I will show you several and let you tell me if any are familiar-looking. By using a picture array, you are not likely to be prejudiced."

"I'll do whatever is necessary to get her in jail, or in the ground. I am ambivalent as to which," Leticia said.

"Let's try for jail. At least we women seem to have a less-er chance of escaping than our outside-plumbed brothers."

Leticia grinned broadly. "Okay, that does it! I love the way you put things. You simply have to participate in one of our tournaments!

"Sounds good. Oh, by the way. Did you exchange any-thing more than names with her?"

"Thank God, nothing but first names. No surnames,

no business cards. Claimed she was an accountant, but I am sure she was lying about that. Didn't match up. But, the good thing is there is no way to track me back home."

"I don't want to make you paranoid. But, kind of watch your rearview mirror for someone who seems to be behind you for too long. Make three right turns. If they are still back there, call 911. And, remember, she will be in a different car this time, too."

"I don't scare easily. And, I can go legally armed. And, I will."

"Good! Just be careful. See you soon."

CHAPTER 8

Sara looked at her watch when she got back in the car from standing at Leticia's Audi to make sure she got away all right. It was four in the morning. By the time she got back to her house at a more normal speed than that which had brought her to Naples, it would be time to go to work.

And, that is what she decided to do. Go home, take a quick shower, go into the office and talk with Maura, then go home and try to get some rest. This case was a night investigation from the start, so she needed to adjust her schedule to that end. She went back into the club to go to the bathroom; now that she had gone to the club in an official capacity and with her badge and gun in plain sight, the option of going for fun without managers, bouncers or patrons knowing what she did for a living had expired. She looked in the mirror while washing her hands. She looked tired, but the shirt and pants had been clean and her ponytail hid the fact she could use a little work on her hair. She decided to go straight to the office, then shower and sleep afterwards.

Sara chatted for a few minutes with the bouncer ne "security officer" and the manager, then got into the Charger and left. Her profession was clearly blown for her next personal visit.

She pulled into the office around six and immediately brewed a pot of coffee. The common joke is cops living on doughnuts or bagels. Actually, they lived on coffee. And, too many added cigarettes to the equation. At least that was a habit she had not ever acquired.

Upon checking emails, she found one from Maura from six-thirty the night before. Just the time sent suggested that the new crime analyst may be later coming in this morning, so she needed to leave notes for her instead of having a face-to-face.

The actual content of the email from Maura said that her call to Louisa Love had been successful and that Louisa would be sitting down with a GBI sketch artist today off premises. The artist, once a likeness was agreed upon, would then computer-age Allen Douglas by ten years. This was exactly the topic about which Sara wanted to speak with Maura.

In view of recent events, she wondered if the artist could also do a rendition of Allen as a female with blonde hair. Sara put that in the reply email and sent one more message. This one was to the LT, telling him she had been in Naples all night, updating him on the case and said she needed to get some rest in case tonight was the same. She copied her two companion detectives.

A serial killer case was big and this one had now grown to be Sheriff's Office-wide, instead of her just doing her usual thing. Her concern was that, soon, the FDLE and feds would get into it and it would be out of control. If their manpower and money stopped the killings, all the better. But, she was not so sure that would be the case. She knew that she was confident, smart and very persistent. Sara identified with Texas Ranger Captain Bill McDonald's quote "No man in the wrong can stand up against a fellow that's in the right and keeps on a-coming." And, she would do just that until this murderer was in handcuffs. She would keep on a-coming.

But, emails read and replied, she was now ready for some rest, since she had slept less than two hours in the last twenty-four. She went back to her house, ate a protein bar, brushed her teeth and went to bed, her phone beside her face.

Sara slept until two, then arose, put on gym clothes and took her other clothes and gear with her to the small gym at the Sheriff's Office. She worked out for forty-five minutes, legs, arms and core, showered and was back at her desk meeting with Maura. The crime analyst had the first iteration of a sketch of Allen Douglas, Allen aged by ten years, and Allen as a woman aged by ten years. The pictures were remarkably detailed. She had promised Leticia Foreman an array. But, she was unable to come up with any sketches that were close in style or physical characteristics.

"Hello, Leticia? This is Sara Nichols. First off, how are you feeling?"

"Hi, Sara. I am sore as hell. I am on the boat making some final preparations and will be going to the captain's meeting and dinner in about an hour. Got anything new?"

"I do. I have a sketch of a suspect, one of him computer-aged to the current time, and one of him aged as a woman to the current time. I promised an array, but I cannot find anything close enough to create one. I'd really like for you to look at the woman."

"I'm nowhere near a fax machine."

"How big is the screen on your phone?"

"Not very. But, I have my iPad on the boat with me. I use it to take fish pictures and recordings."

"Can I text to it?"

"Yes, it's set up for that."

"This number? Good! Stand by and I will take a cell phone photo and text it. It won't be ideal, but you are the only one I can rely on right now for any sort of identity guidance."

Sara took a picture and texted it to Leticia.

Leticia studied it full screen on the tablet and called her back.

"I'm sorry, Sara. But, that is not anything like Allie. I mean, the hair is probably the same color as what was under the wig—hard to tell, of course in black and white on a fax, but the nose is wrong and the face is too long. Maybe in the dark from a distance, someone would mistake her for this picture, but not up close."

"Crap! I was hoping, but at least we went through the exercise. The next step is for us to have an artist do a sketch based on *your* memory of Allie. I will contact you about that as soon as I have it set up. Have fun tonight and good luck tomorrow! I hope to see your picture by the winner board in the local paper."

"Thanks, Sara. It should be a good day. Bye."

Maura was sitting at Sara's desk listing to the conversation.

"Not the answer we wanted, but it's what we got, so we'll work with it," Maura said.

"You know, Maura, if these two sets of murders—Georgia and Florida ten years apart—had any sort of publicity connecting them, I'd say we had a copycat. But, they don't have any way a copycat could know about...unless, he or she was in Georgia then."

"Well, a good thing that has come out of your actions so far is that the Georgia case has been reopened. I still think, Sara, that when one is solved, the other will be, too."

"That just has to be the case. I am going to see if Detective Cruz has access to a sketch artist in Naples, which I doubt. If not, I will get one and take him or her down there to work with Leticia."

She took Cruz' card out of her case file and dialed him; Maura went back to her cubicle and started to put the three attacks so far on a "murder board" so they could try detect relationships visually that might not jump out from verbal representations.

Cruz did not have immediate access to an artist, so Sara called one she knew and got a couple of possible times in the next few days to check against Leticia's schedule. The Naples detective did send her the transcript of the interviews he and his officers had done at the night club the night of the attack against Leticia.

His bad news was that the driver of the Jaguar had succumbed to the injuries she received when Allie had struck her. His traffic case had escalated to vehicular homicide. The damaged car had been found in a canal and had been emptied and wiped clean.

On a side note, he told Sara that the deceased woman had been the trophy wife of a sixty-something Marco Island millionaire who had no idea that she had preferences other than for him. Cruz said there was quite a scandal surrounding what should have been a sad, tragic event.

Sara looked at the situation with as much equanimity as she could, but finally decided that the great preponderance of people thought too much with emotions and not enough with logic and understanding.

She called Leticia with the times and then called the artist back and confirmed Sunday, after the fishing tournament.

The retired GBI agent called and gave Sara the name and contact number of his successor, as well as that agent's interest in working together on the twin serial killer cases.

She had some home burglary cases to work on until she had the sketch artist ready to take to Leticia, or the killer struck again. Sara felt that things were going as well as they could, given the relative lack of clues...at least clues that corresponded with each other in a way to lead to a quick solution of the cases.

Sara had just received a list, with pictures and serial numbers, where relevant, from State Farm Insurance. The items were the "take" from a residential burglary that had occurred last week. She decided to make copies and physically hand them to pawn shop managers in the county. She had a list of twenty. While the usual way would be to mail them or fax them, she believed in the personal touch whenever possible.

She slid the marker next to her name on the board outside the LT's office to "OUT" and left with an envelope full of copies.

By the fifth pawn shop, she had a hit. A three-thousand-dollar engraved Colt Python revolver had been brought in. The pawn shop owner had the thumb print and surveillance footage. He said the male subject had "weird eyes," probably strung out on something. Sara left him his copy and took possession of the gun.

She called a relieved owner but said they may have to keep it for evidence through the trial once she caught the guy. The doper's name was Joe Tracor and some work with the increasingly indispensable Maura provided his vehicle description, home with Google Earth photos in a mobile home community and a lengthy petty crime rap sheet, but with one felony conviction.

Sara went to the lieutenant's office and presented her arrest plan to him. She and one detective, with several SWAT operators would drop in on Mr. Tracor for a chat. She said the latter were prudent because a number of shotguns and shells were still missing and he might be heavily armed. The LT agreed and immediately called the SWAT sergeant. Sara and Cindy would conduct surveillance. Once Tracor was spotted, they would call in SWAT for the take-down. She immediately went over to the court and swore out an arrest warrant with the magistrate, based on the pawn shop film and the thumbprint verified to be Tracor's.

Sara called Cindy and they agreed to meet at an Arby's near the mobile home park where Tracor lived. She shared the plan with Cindy over Jamoka shakes. They took both unmarked cars to the park and stopped short of Tracor's trailer. His old F-150 truck was parked outside. She got on the radio to the SWAT sergeant and told him the subject was probably there and she was holding an arrest warrant. Osprey SWAT deputies, or in the case of Bob Axelrod, who was a detective with SWAT collateral duties, went about normal assignments with their SWAT gear in their vehicles, awaiting a call-out. On large or pre-planned events, one of several heavy SWAT vehicles would be deployed. That was unlikely to be the case with this burglar, unless he decided to become a "barricaded subject."

The office for the mobile home park was not in sight of Tracor's trailer. Sara and Cindy went in and provided ID to a shifty-looking manager. They verified that only Tracor and a male roommate lived there and there would be no children present. While Cindy stayed inside watching the manager to make sure he did not call and warn Tracor, Sara stepped out and called the SWAT sergeant and informed him.

In five minutes, SWAT would come into the park at as high a speed as prudent and stop in front of the trailer. They had Sara's Google Earth photos and Sara would be in the lead vehicle to point them to the proper trailer, while Cindy stayed with the manager until SWAT was on scene.

On cue, the sergeant and Sara in a SWAT pickup and three SUVs roared in and stopped in front of Tracor's trailer. The operators bailed out and hit the door with an announcement and a knock. No answer, so they used a short-barreled breeching shotgun load to destroy the lock and went in fast and hard.

Since the trailer was small, they appeared within a minute with two males in boxers and sleeveless undershirts. Both appeared strung out and half asleep.

The second one out was Tracor. Sara went up to him

with the warrant and arrested him for felony burglary. A SWAT operator found jeans and shoes for the two and the clothes were quickly checked for weapons and drugs. It was apparent that the two were unarmed in their underwear, but they were searched anyway.

Sara and Cindy searched the small trailer. They found two loaded guns from the burglary where the expensive Colt had been taken. Being a felon with a firearm would land him an additional federal charge. She would call the Bureau of Alcohol, Tobacco, Firearms & Explosives once they got back to the office.

Drugs had been included in the search warrant, and they were rewarded by a cache of meth.

There was an aluminum shed outside with a padlock. The SWAT sergeant used his bolt cutter on it. Inside, they found the rest of the guns and ammunition and some electronics that corresponded to a different robbery. It was all inventoried, bagged and tagged as evidence, and put in one of the SWAT SUVs.

Dressed now, the two were put in one of the SWAT deputy's SUVs after the search and taken to the Sheriff's Office.

Back at the office, the two were handcuffed to bolted-down chairs in separate interview rooms and left to cogitate about life for an hour. During that time, Sara, Cindy, Maura and Mary Higgins separated the evidence by robbery and noted the robbery address and dates on the evidence tags. Mary then photographed all and pictures were placed in the appropriate case files.

"Maura and Mary. Cindy and I are going to interview these two brain trusts separately. Do you want to watch from the video room and see what you can pick up on facial expression and body language?"

"Sure!" said Maura for both.

"Before we do that, Mary. Please get a rap sheet on John

Wilson. Here is his Florida driver's license and a Social Security card."

Mary was back in ten minutes with a lengthy history of violent and property crime that well exceeded Tracor's record. Sara could use that for leverage.

The two detectives went into the interview room where Wilson, the second subject was being held.

"All right. This interview is commencing on," Sara looked at her watch then spoke the time and date, "I am Detective Sara Nichols. This is Detective Cynthia Leton. The person being interviewed is John Estes Wilson." She then gave his address and Social Security Number.

"Mr. Wilson, I believe you see the prominent sign on the wall across from you that says this room is recorded for video and sound. That is for your protection."

"The first thing we are going to do is to read you your rights to not self-incriminate. These are commonly known as the Miranda Rights. Then, we will get you to sign that you were read the rights, understood them and decided to, or not to, waive the rights. So, let's get going"

Cindy began," You have the right to remain silent, you have the right to have an attorney present during this or any future interview. Should you wish an attorney, but be unable to afford one, the court will appoint one at no cost to you. Do you understand these rights as I have explained them to you?" Wilson nodded affirmatively. "Mr. Wilson, I need a verbal response. Do you understand these rights, yes or no?"

"Yeah."

"Do you wish to waive your rights?"

"Yeah. I been through this before. Had real bad luck with a public defender. Better using my own gut."

"Okay, please sign here that you have been read the rights and here that you have decided to waive them."

He signed both places.

"Please state your full name again for the record," Cindy asked. He did.

"Mr. Wilson, you live in a trailer home with one Joseph Edward Tracor. Is that correct?"

"Yes."

"Have you assisted or led Mr. Tracor in any burglaries in Osprey County, or elsewhere?"

Wilson paused. Sara and Cindy could see the wheels turning.

Sara spoke.

"Mr. Wilson, carefully consider your answer. Your record shows that, by Florida statutory definition, you are a three-time loser and will get the maximum sentence. Also, while you have been sitting in here, Mr. Tracor has been spilling his guts. He has told us that you are the leader in these robberies and that you have participated in all of them. Now, the answer please."

Cindy interjected. "I think we ought to help him if he meets us halfway. You know, if he incriminates, Tracor, we ask the State's Attorney to reduce his charge. Or, maybe not enforce the 'three times and you are screwed' statute."

"No, I don't think so. We have enough on him already to put him away. Remember, we have two sets of prints at one or two of the houses," Sara lied. She was well aware of the US Supreme Court decision in Frazier v. Cupp that affirmed the legality of police using deception in interrogation.

They could see that Wilson was becoming agitated. He blurted out.

"We did it together. Nobody was the boss. We needed money for drugs. That's all. We didn't hurt nobody."

"How many burglaries?"

"Three."

"All in Osprey?"

"Yeah."

"Other than the Colt revolver, have you sold other goods you took in the burglaries?"

"Yes. We sold some electronics at the trailer court. The rest was in the shed. I told that asshole Tracor to not sell the gun at a pawn shop, but, no. Would he listen? Hell, no!"

Sara said "Okay, you have met us halfway, so we will let the State's Attorney know that. What we'd like for you to do is take this pad and write out what you told us—we will help with form, but it will be in your words. Start with the first burglary, the who-what-why-where and when, then do the same thing for the others. Then, sign it and date it. Again, we want it in your words, but will help you along."

That process took about an hour to get the detailed confession they wanted. Given that, the interview with Tracor would be shorter and simpler. And, it was. By late afternoon, they had two solid confessions in the hands of the prosecutor. They dropped by the lieutenant's office and advised him the case was closed, except for any required testimony by detectives at trial.

"I love it when a good plan comes together!" he told them.

"That means the two of us are your 'A-team,' right, Hannibal?"

He grinned. "I loved that show. Even the later movie was pretty good. Yeah, but we've got to add everybody and call it the best A-team around!"

Cindy responded, "That's good with us, LT." The two detectives high-fived and went back to their respective cubicles.

Sara called Lynn.

"This is the detective who just got two confessions and closed the case on a series of burglaries. All stolen goods recovered. Perps in jail. So, I feel like buying some friend drinks and dinner at the Salty Snook. Know anybody who might be interested?"

"Is this really Sara? I thought I heard something about 'buying drinks and dinner?' That doesn't sound like something my good friend would have come out of her mouth."

"It is I and I am serious. Say 'yes' and a time and I will make reservations. I may even go home and put on girly-girl clothes to celebrate in."

"Does this mean you will take me on a Caribbean cruise when you crack the serial killer case?"

"You know, that will be such a big deal, such a thing is not beyond the realm of possibility."

"Wow! Would you consider putting that in writing?"

"Probably not."

"Okay, then. Send me a text as to when for dinner. I will be there and absolutely stunning, as usual."

"Of course you will be. Let me get some reservations. I'll text. Bye!"

"Bye."

Sara got reservations for six-thirty and texted her friend the time to meet. Both had to take their official vehicles, since both were perpetually on call. Sara showered, played with the cats and fed them, then put on a pink and lime green flowered sundress and pink sandals. She managed to get her badge case, handcuffs, a pistol magazine, flashlight and her gun in a matching bag. It was not easy. She kept a nylon raid jacket, golf shirt, slacks, socks and spare running shoes in the trunk of the Charger in case she needed them.

She left for the restaurant, brown hair long and not tied back and looking very good, she thought. Sara felt a little overshadowed when the medical examiner showed up, dressed similarly, but more expensively. Sara was not at all jealous; she knew she was eye-catchingly pretty, but that Lynn was absolutely beautiful, and that was okay.

"Hiya, Foxy Doc. You are looking special tonight."

"And, you are too, Xena!"

They were taken straight to their table on the water-front. As they drank Sea Breezes, they watched long, sleek performance boats, offshore center consoles and sports fishing cruisers come and go in the harbor. It made Sara long to go back to the Keys and visit her brother's family and get on the water in something larger than her kayak and stand up paddle board, or SUP.

Making sure no one could overhear, Lynn asked softly, "What's going on with the big case? Anything new?"

"No. I thought it was a male. Now, a female matching the description of my POI has attacked a woman at a club in Naples. And, killed an innocent bystander with her car."

"So, it's a woman. I would not have guessed that."

"Me either, Lynn."

"What now?"

"I don't know. I'm in a quandary. I don't want to wait for the other shoe to drop. Sunday, I am taking a sketch artist to draw the blonde's likeness from the memory of the victim who got away. I will personally take that to every lesbian and gay night club and bar in a several county radius. Maybe we can get a call when she walks in instead of walking out with a victim, then killing her. I hope so."

"Me, too, though it is good for my business."

"Good thing you are so attractive, being as macabre as you are."

"Isn't it ever?"

Dinner came. Sara had Chilean sea bass and Lynn had snow crab claws. It was excellent. They were about to order dessert, when Sara got a call.

"Detective Nichols."

"Yes, Sara. This is Leticia. I am at the Redfish Inn at the captain's meeting for tomorrow's tournament. I swear I just saw the blonde, bruise and all. She disappeared after we saw each other. Should I be scared?"

"Well, you should be careful. If she's at that type event, she is probably looking for you. Luckily the Inn is in southernmost Osprey. I will fill the area with deputies. I'd love a car description if you could get another captain or two to get it. I don't want you trying, unless you are in a crowd of protectors, okay?"

"No problem with that here!" Leticia said.

"Leticia? I changed my mind—you stay seated with as tough a group of captains as you can. Tell them what's going on. Let some of them get a car description and tags, okay? Stay there until you see a deputy walk in."

"I sure as hell will with this crazy razor bitch on the prowl!"

She hung up. Lynn had overheard half the conversation and had already summoned the server. She paid the bill as Sara sprinted for her car. She sat with the engine running while she put out the call for deputies twenty miles away to respond to the restaurant. She said for the first one to go in and watch for Leticia to signal to him or her.

As Sara was finishing the radio transmission, Lynn got into the front of the Charger with her medical bag.

"Sara, you don't want me to drive this thing while you change from girly-girl to cop?"

"No time! I will slip on a raid jacket and running shoes when I get there!"

"Good idea. A boob almost came out when you ran out the door. A guy at the bar almost choked. I thought I was going to have to do the Heimlich Maneuver."

"Glad you didn't. We didn't have time for you to save a boob watcher."

"Hell, girl. Everybody's a boob watcher, not just leering guys. Even girls like to see a surprise tittie every now and then!"

"This is going to be fast. Sure you don't want to take your coroner car and follow?"

"Punch it, Danno. We are friends, I can handle anything you got!"

Sara stayed on the busier Tamiami Trail instead of going far east to the Interstate. They made good time for a busy state route on a Friday night. Five minutes before she pulled in, she heard Sgt. Joe Fletcher put out a call for all units to watch for a white Toyota minivan and gave an approximate quadrant. Less than thirty minutes later, Sara parked illegally at the restaurant between two marked deputy units from OCSO.

They got out. As Sara popped the trunk and slipped on the nylon raid jacket that said SHERIFF on front and back in large yellow letters and running shoes, the ME observed "I always thought driving like that would be fun. It's not is it?"

"Sometimes in no traffic it is. Most of the times, it's not fun."

Sara saw Sgt. Joe Fletcher and a South District deputy. The rest, per her radio call and his subsequent one, were combing the area.

The sergeant looked up and motioned her over to where he was talking with Leticia and a group of fishing guides, or so they appeared.

"Sara, we may have something," he said as she approached.

"Detective Sara Nichols, this is Capt. Woody Woodson. He's a former Green Beret and followed the blonde to the parking lot. She got into a white Toyota minivan. The license was muddied, probably on purpose."

"Good job, Captain! Thanks."

As she spoke with Leticia about the circumstances of seeing the blonde woman, she heard an urgent radio call come in over the radio on the sergeant's belt.

"Radio! This is 1302. I am in pursuit of a white Toyota van south on I-75. Stand by for a mile marker. Request backup!"

Sara tossed the keys for the Charger to Lynn. "I'll ride with Joe in his marked unit. You want to bring Leticia and follow at normal speeds in the Charger?" Lynn nodded and Sara, Joe and the deputy, who was new to the County, quickly headed for cars.

"1302! I am still southbound. Speeds over one hundred. Subject vehicle is driving erratically."

"1302, this is 3018. Suspend pursuit and follow with no lights," the sergeant radioed.

"1302 copies."

"Radio, 3018. Do we have Air up?"

"Negative on helicopter, Sergeant."

"Osprey or highway patrol units south for a roadblock?"

"1247! I am south of 1302's last called position by five miles. I have an FHP unit running with me. We can set up a block."

"1247, this is 3018. Do it!"

"Copy!"

Sara knew what Joe had done. He was fearful of causing a multiple car accident and decided to end the pursuit and stop the vehicle by a safer method.

Three minutes later, the southernmost unit advised that he and the highway patrol car had set up a roadblock and he gave the mile marker.

"1247 from 3018: do either of you have stop sticks?"

"Negative."

"1247, this is a homicide suspect. If she does not stop and you can take out the tires without endangering other motorists, you have a green light."

"1247. I copy. Both units here have shotguns out. We will use those if we have to."

"1302 from 3018: do you still have a visual on the van?"

I am still southbound running about ninety with no emergency equipment energized. I saw her up until about two minutes ago, still southbound." He gave a mile marker.

"1247! Subject vehicle approaching at high speed! She's not going to stop!"

As the van approached the white with green deputy car and the black and yellow state trooper car parked nose to nose in the center of the road, the driver swerved onto the median. Both officers waited for a clear shot, then each put two loads of buckshot into the van's front tire.

The tire virtually exploded, sending the van out of control. It veered left, then right, going back onto the empty Interstate behind the roadblock and rolling twice. It came to a rest on the shoulder, spinning wheels pointing towards the stars.

"1247! Vehicle has T/A'd. Request fire/rescue immediately!"

At this call, all responding vehicles resumed Code-3, including the ME driving Sara's car. Lynn that she would be needed, either as a physician, or as a coroner.

Lynn made good time and arrived only minutes behind Sara and the sergeant. She knew Sara had a full first aid kit in the trunk and grabbed it before fast-walking to the accident scene.

Allie had not worn a seat belt, but had somehow not been ejected as the van rolled. She had, however, been tossed at high velocity back and forth and appeared grievously injured.

The roadblock deputy and trooper had gotten the driver door open. Allie was laying crumpled on the ceiling of the upside-down vehicle. They were squatting down speaking with her as Sara, then Lynn arrived.

"Don't move her unless there is a fire danger!" The ME ordered. "Let's let the paramedics brace her and use a backboard."

She saw a bit of blood running from the corners of the woman's mouth. Lynn knew it could be from a blow to the face from the rolling of the car, but suspected it might signal internal injuries.

Lynn opened the first aid kit and took out two pairs of blue Nitrile gloves and handed one pair to Sara and put the other pair on.

Lynn started to scan for and itemize wounds. Sara spoke to the victim.

"Hi. My name is Sara. This is Lynn. She is a doctor. We have paramedics coming and will get you to a hospital by helicopter."

Lynn said, "What's your name?"

The blonde woman was in and out of consciousness. She opened her eyes and said "Allie."

"Allie, where do you hurt?"

"Everywhere."

Lynn looked at Sara. Sara could tell from the look that "everywhere" could mean anything, or nothing."

Sara asked, "Allie, what's your last name?"

"Cooper."

"Did you know Rose Douglas?"

"Bitch. Die. All of them. Die!"

"All of who, Allie?"

"All Roses."

"Allie, do you know Allen Douglas?"

Allie looked at her and closed her eyes.

Lynn checked her pulse. She was still alive, but she feared shock had set in and she could be in big trouble, unless she got critical care. She turned to the sergeant.

"Please start the process for a medevac by helicopter."

Joe Fletcher keyed his radio and requested it, even before paramedics arrived.

Sara looked at Lynn and Joe. "'All Roses die'. Everyone connected with Rose? Everyone who looked like Rose? How does she know Rose? We are so close, but so far."

Allie, eyes closed, smiled. It was almost angelic. She said nothing and lapsed into what could have been a coma.

Sara looked around the totaled van and found Allie's purse. She took possession and put it in the Charger for review later and contact of next-of-kin.

Other responding troopers and deputies cordoned off an area for the landing zone. Paramedics arrived and with the doctor's oversight, packaged Allie Cooper for medevac. She was still alive, but non-communicative, when the helicopter took off. Despite being a longer flight, it headed towards Tampa General, the closest Level One Trauma Center to the scene.

Sara had Joe secure the van and call the CSI team to look at it for fingerprints and any other possible clues. Once he had a deputy tape it off and stand guard by it, he began organizing things for the shooting team that would review what had happened. It was a "clean" shoot, but procedures had to be followed.

Sara and Lynn got back in the Charger and went back to the restaurant where Lynn's vehicle was. Sara went in and changed to her normal daily wear from the extra clothes in the trunk.

Since she was making the trip to Tampa General. Lynn decided not to go, but asked that, if Allie died, to have her sent to Osprey County for her autopsy.

Sara hit I-75 North and accelerated the car. She had more questions than answers.

CHAPTER 9

Sara arrived at Tampa General Hospital two hours later. The information that Allie Cooper was a multiple homicide suspect and was Sara's arrestee was communicated upon the helicopter's arrival to the roof of the hospital.

Allie was still in Intensive Care when Sara arrived. She learned that, miraculously, the woman did not receive organic internal injuries during the rollover but did receive several sprains and contusions and still had her eyes closed and was not responding. She was not considered by the hospital to be a threat sufficient to be restrained to her bed, but there was a Tampa PD officer outside the room…for now.

Allie's purse held a wallet which had the normal collection of licenses and credit cards and store cards for supermarkets and pharmacies. There was no insurance card. The van was stolen, but the key was in the switch, so either she hijacked it or bought it from an addict like the previous car. The owner had not been located by the Osprey Sheriff's Office yet.

As she sat in the waiting room, Sara went through the cards. Using Safari on her smart phone, she traced the supermarkets down to an area of Georgia north of Thomasville by some seventy miles. She would communicate all the information to Maura on Monday to try to get some vital statistics information, like a birth certificate. A suspicion was growing in Sara's mind, based on what Allie had said before she passed out...or faked passing out.

The medical team came out of the room and Sara walked to them, directing them out of hearing of Allie's room.

"I'm Osprey County Detective Sara Nichols. Ms. Cooper is my prisoner. She's the suspect in multiple homicides. I am working on identifying next of kin, but no luck yet. Can you tell me something about her condition?"

A doctor spoke. "She is injured, but very lucky. Some severely strained joints and contusions from being tossed about in the accident, but no serious internal injuries— maybe some bruising inside, but no ruptures of organs."

"Good, doctor. A physician on scene thought there might be internal injuries from bleeding at the mouth."

"I would have probably thought same thing. She bit the inside of her cheek during the tumbling around."

"She seemed to lapse into a coma after talking briefly..." Sara began.

"There is no indication of her being comatose. No brain swelling or injuries to the skull."

"Could she be faking a coma then?"

"Well, she can't fake it medically, but she could give a good performance, if she was so inclined, to lay persons."

"I'm leaning towards playing along with her and seeing what her game is."

"That's between you and her. We will just treat her based on her needs."

"She is dangerous and a flight risk. Is her condition such that she can be restrained as of this time?"

"I don't see why not."

The doctor, several nurses, and Sara walked back to the officer sitting outside the door and obtained and fastened a handcuff to the bed's rail. Dealing with prisoners was something with which TGH had frequent experience.

"I will let the hospital staff know when we have next of kin information. I have insurance information to give to you all now."

"We usually hold all the purse contents."

"Not when it's evidence in a multiple homicide case, doctor."

"Guess not."

They went on to check on other patients and Sara, after assuring herself Allie would be under live guard, even after the restraints had been added, still walked back in. No booking pictures had been made, so she snapped a quick cell phone photo of Allie and checked it. Not bad. She was pretty sure that Allie would not answer any questions, so decided to let her stew in her juices overnight, and left.

On the slower drive back down I-75, Sara found herself thinking about relationships, not cases. She and Lynn had a wonderful relationship, but had both agreed it was too good to mess with. Both dated others and compared notes without any hint of jealousy. Sara's biggest impediment to relationships was her time and her job. She hardly had time to plan dates and, quite frankly, many women were put off by her being a detective. She knew that male officers had the same problem and that is why they often ended up with female cops, firefighters or nurses—people who understood the demands of the job and had similar demand and time constraints themselves. Lynn kind of fit in that paradigm. Maybe one day, they would combine households and change the nature of their relationship. She could love Lynn. She probably already did. But, for now, BFF and sex partner worked just fine. For now, …

She also thought about Sally. Hot Sally and the perfect smokin' body. But, perhaps too widely traveled on the swinging lesbian circuit, if one actually existed or was created one alliance at a time. She would be a great one-night stand, assuming she had not been with bi's who may have picked up some things from male partners that Sara would like to avoid. Leticia, too, was interesting. Independent, and she liked a lot of the outdoorsy things that Sara liked. She would give some thought there, after the case was closed, and see where that led.

Sara then gave some thought to how Sally would be in bed. Then, how Leticia would be. Then, how both would be. That made her blush a bit, but she carried the thought out to its completion. Normally, such detailed fantasies would have aroused her to need some satisfaction. But, tonight she was just too exhausted. Maybe later.

******

The man in the van had monitored the radio traffic about the roadblock and had even gotten into the tail-end of the parking lot of cars on I-75, stopped due to first the roadblock, then second, the crash and Allie's helicopter medevac. He saw the helicopter head north, leaving a plethora of Ft. Myers, Sarasota, St. Petersburg and Tampa choices without even consulting the Internet. He thought that a helicopter transport would likely signal the need for a trauma center and narrowed that down to several. He had his work cut out for him.

******

Allie suspected that the IV drip had a combination of things, including the painkiller that was making her feel far better than she knew she should. She watched the clock on the wall, then shut her eyes when she heard movement. The cop on guard stuck his head in her door for a second every fifteen minutes. As near as she could tell, he had gone through fourteen iterations of checking without a movement on her part. That was good.

She eased the needle out of her arm and used it to pick the lock on her handcuffs. Allie was careful to not clink the metal against the bar on her hospital bed. She heard the officer speaking with someone in the hall and used that noise to mask the sound of her using the remote to lower both the bar and the bed. He would be coming in to check in eight minutes. Predictability gets people killed, she thought. Allie looked around the room for something heavy; she did not want to take on a burly male cop un-armed and in a weakened condition. She was not even sure how she would handle standing up. There was no blunt object obvious in the room. She reached into the cabinet door below her bedside table. Her clothes, as per procedure, were in a brown paper bag. The expensive heels were there and she picked up one, holding it like a hammer, with the three-inch heel pointed downwards. It would have to work; she had nothing else.

Allie put pillows and the blanket under the sheets to somewhat simulate her body to one who has looked many times and seen nothing. She stood beside the door in the hospital gown, her bare rear showing through the back.

She watched the clock. It was time. She heard the chair make a sound as he stood. He must have stretched or scratched his balls or something, because he did not appear instantly.

Then, Allie saw a head lean in. Something about the form in the bed must have seemed amiss, because he leaned further in. She brought the high heel down on the base of his skull as hard as she could and heard something crunch. She was not sure whether it was skull or shoe, until she tried to remove the shoe and it stayed where it was.

Allie caught him as he fell, silencing the fall. She dragged him to the corner and removed his car keys, gun and a tactical folding knife, something she would need for the last two on her list. She pulled on her pants and blouse. Allie used the hospital slippers, since she was down to one shoe. She looked at the man crumpled in the corner, wondering if one had killed seven people, whether adding a cop would make her be executed any more times. She put the gun and knife in the bag that had held her clothes.

She looked down the hall. There were several nurses at the station, talking and watching monitoring equipment. She slipped out towards the stair exit and pulled the fire alarm on the way by. Before anyone could turn, she was in the stairwell, heading down, alarm blaring and strobe lights flickering in the ceiling throughout the hospital.

At the bottom, she looked at the cop's car keys. They were Chevrolet keys. Allie went to the rear of the hospital and looked for an area marked "Police Parking." No luck. She held up the key and pressed the "Lock" button. Walking around the back of the hospital, she continued to do that until she heard a horn beep. It was a marked unit. How fun! Allie got in and left, pulling around arriving fire trucks.

It would be a little while before they found the dead officer and figured out his car was gone. She needed to head towards the rooming house fifty miles south, where her clothes and travel supplies were. But, the car would have to be ditched soon.

Allie watched a Mercedes as it pulled to a stop beside her. As it pulled away when the light changed, she reached down and hit the switch named "Light Bar." She could see the reflection in the store fronts. She saw "PA" on another switch, flipped it and picked up the mic.

"Tampa Police! Make your next right turn at the alley, pull in and stop!"

The terrified woman did so. Allie got out, holding the pistol out of sight at her side and approached the car.

"Put the car in Park and step out, please!"

"What kind of cop are you, dressed like that?"

"Undercover vice. Step to the other side of your car now!"

The woman did and Allie shot her between the eyes. She walked back to the police car and turned the red and blue lights off. Then, she switched the mic back to radio and screamed into it, "Officer down! Officer needs assistance!" She knew that the call would wreak havoc, especially without a location. She hoped there was no homing device to tie the call back to this car and its present location, but she was going to be gone in her new Mercedes anyway, with a hopefully full purse and wallet on the passenger seat.

As she sped through a rough section of Tampa, characterized by public housing and lots of young men hanging around corners, their boxers showing over baggy jeans worn down below their asses, an idea began to form.

Allie spotted four. Several vehicles were pulled into the curb. She knew that vehicle ownership in places like this was by possession more than registration card or bill of sale. Cars and trucks passed from person to person like lovers. One of the vehicles was a compact Toyota pickup, maybe six years old, but not bad looking.

The blonde woman swerved into the corner, scattering young males. She quickly dropped the magazine out of the cop's gun and wiped it down before pointing it at her new friends.

"Hello, boys! How'd you like to trade this new Mercedes even for that pickup? The Mercedes is paid for."

She pointed the forty-caliber automatic at the crotch of an eighteen-year old who was reaching in his pocket.

"I'm getting the keys, dammit!"

"Ease 'em out or you are going to be a girl in a second. A girl in a world of pain."

He did.

"Get in and start it!"

As soon as she heard it running, she asked, "How much gas in the tank?"

He looked down and said, "Half."

"Now, get your sorry ass out and come look at your new Benz. And, you get two bonuses: one, you get to keep your balls."

As she got in the truck and buckled in, he asked "What's the other bonus?"

"This!" She tossed him the pistol. He fumbled for it and ended up pointing it at her.

"Won't shoot without a magazine in it. Magazine to the pistol and the car keys are in the back floorboard some-where, assholes!" Allie gunned the Toyota and sped off as the men scrambled to the rear door of the Mercedes to look for both.

Allie smiled. She now had a vehicle that probably would not be reported stolen, unless he had just stolen it himself from a legitimate, certificate of registration-holding owner, which seemed unlikely to her. And, the murder weapon was in the hands of a guy who she suspected had already put his drug dealer's prints all over it. She had quickly smeared whatever prints she had left on the grip before tossing it to him. She had confused the cops big time.

As she was driving away, the four were already climbing into the Mercedes to take it to a lot behind some houses. It would not be seen from the street and they could check it out better. Also, they knew that the woman was crazy and might just call the cops on them for the fun of it, so they wanted it out of sight for a few days. Allie could not have planned that better.

******

At three in the morning, Sara got a call about an escape, a dead police officer, a fire alarm, a stolen police car, a carjacked Mercedes and a dead society matron. Allie had graduated from serial killer to crime wave.

She had Dispatch put out a BOLO describing the person and the car, which had been determined to be a tan S-Class, a large Mercedes sedan. Sara wondered whether she should go back up to Tampa and raise hell over them losing her prisoner. But, they had lost something more. A police officer officer. She was sure that a command post would be set up. She had her Dispatch call Tampa PD to determine where and got dressed. It was going to be a long day. She called both Sally and Leticia, awakening both, to warn them about Allie being on the loose again. Allie had been medevac'd, not arrested, so there was no booking photo for searching officers to use. Sara mouthed every dirty word she could think of and made up a few that she liked and might claim ownership of. The process did not make her feel any better, unfortunately, so she drove northwards, her mouth tightly shut.

Osprey dispatch had found out that the command post vehicle was at the hospital, so she drove there.

A haggard sergeant greeted her at the door of the motorhome converted to command post.

He looked at her badge, gun and Osprey Sheriff's Office on her shirt.

"Help you?"

"Other way around. I'm here to help you. That was my prisoner who escaped. Who's in charge?"

"Oh, that's why your shirt rang a bell. It's been a long, crappy night. There is a captain inside. Introduce yourself to her."

Sara walked in. The captain turned. While they had never met, it was apparent that they had something in common.

"Hey."

"Hi, Captain. I'm Sara Nichols from Osprey County. The prisoner was mine. Sorry about your officer. Maybe I can help, since I'm a little familiar with her."

"Yeah, a picture would help."

Sara got her phone out. "You up on the Internet in here?"

"I am."

"What's your email?"

"It's my name, Rikki Lawson, with the TPD tag on the end," which she proceeded to give to Sara. Sara emailed her the photo she had taken of Allie.

"She must not have been hurt as badly as all of us, doctors included, thought," Sara said.

"I wondered about that, so I asked her doc. He said that she *was* badly hurt, but that they had pumped her full of painkillers in the IV. She is going to feel awful in about an hour, he said."

"Maybe she will get sloppy and wreck the Mercedes," Sara said.

"We should be so lucky. We found the owner near the stolen police car. One shot. Dead. Wealthy older lady. This woman is mean."

"Captain, counting the Mercedes woman and your officer, I am looking at her for possibly ten homicides in Georgia, Southwest Florida and Tampa."

"That means we will be overrun with feds. Everybody is going to want to get a piece of this for the six o'clock news."

"True. Unfortunately, unless we get really lucky, that cannot be helped."

"I know. Still pisses me off."

"Me, too, Captain."

"Rikki."

Sara stuck out her hand, "Sara."

Rikki gave her a firm grip and said, "Yeah, got it."

"Rikki, to go with the picture for your BOLO, she is tall and has a great figure—thin with big bosom—and light blonde hair. She's a looker. Mid-thirties probably."

"What's her connection to the other murders? I read about the ones in your area. Sounds like lesbians."

"That is true in Florida. We don't know if it is with the Georgia women she allegedly killed after murdering a madam at a brothel. I still like the madam's son for those five. But, here, one was a vehicular homicide when her last attempted murder went awry. But, she was a lady getting out of her car at a lesbian night club in Naples, so that counts. Both knifings were lesbians. She was connected to both through meeting at a club in Ft. Myers. So, all of mine are lesbians. The madam in Georgia was bi. The connection is razor to the throat and leaving virtually no trace."

"That's hard to do. Anybody looked into whether she is or was a cop?"

"The GBI agent who had the Georgia end of her spree talked about that, but couldn't get anywhere with it. He and I still think the killer up there is a male and this one is a copycat, and is somehow connected to him or his victims, or hit on the same MO accidentally. Every time I get close, it gets clouded up again."

Rikki was pensive for a minute. "You know, "she began, "I think everything points to her being a cop or military. The picking the lock on the cuffs, accurate use of a handgun, using the lights on the police car to pull the Mercedes and the radio to put out a false call. No evidence. She's good. She may be a psycho, but she is a good one."

"Hmm…let me get our new crime analyst on that. And, the GBI again. This has been just Georgia and Florida as far as we know—yet—so we could make some inquiries about whether a pretty thirty-five-year old female cop was fired, disappeared or something. Also, check VICAP, if we can narrow the search down for their system," Sara proposed. Rikki nodded affirmatively.

Sara sat at a desk and started to thumb an email to Maura into her smart phone, as Rikki passed the photo email to a plain clothes assistant to use in development of a BOLO. That look out presumed that Allie still had the officer's gun and would be armed and dangerous.

Minutes later, she and Rikki Lawson promised to contact one another at the first break in the case, and Sara left for home.

******

The man in the van was tired and generally pissed off. Once he heard the BOLO from Osprey County on his scanner, modified to overcome the county's scrambling, he looked up the digital address for Tampa PD in a small directory he carried. He programmed that in and headed north to Tampa as Allie was pulling into a parking space behind the rooming house where she currently lived.

It did not take him long, by listening to Tampa Police radio, to determine that the place he needed to go was Tampa General Hospital. Unfortunately, he learned, Allie was not there. Where the hell was she?

He parked the van in a dark corner of the hospital parking lot and walked to the command post vehicle, which was basically a motorhome with a red and blue light bar, and police insignias on the outside.

The man knocked on the door and heard a "Come in," from the other side. He went in and saw Rikki and several other officers standing there looking at him suspiciously.

"If you are media, turn around right now. We will have a press conference tomorrow at ten. You don't belong in here."

"No, my name is Douglas. I am a bail enforcement agent. I think your escapee is my skip."

"A bounty hunter?" Rikki asked.

"Yes, Ma'am. That's what we used to be called. When did she get away and how?"

"What court and crime did she skip out on?" Rikki asked, ignoring his questions.

"Murder. South Georgia. She's been on the run for a while."

"Do you know anything about murders here in Florida?"

"No, I don't," he lied.

"There are three women in Southwest Florida and another woman and a Tampa police officer here."

"That's horrible!" he said looking her straight in the eye.

"What do you have in your files on her? How does she get vehicles? Where did she get trained? Does she have any safe houses and where?"

"I don't really know the answers to any of that. I just got handed this case. Training, what do you mean?"

"She seems to have a lot of cop skills. Was she a cop? Military?"

"News to me," he said.

"You can catch her, and we will give you a receipt, but we keep her. She killed our officer. She's gonna damn well pay for that here in Hillsborough County. So, good luck, but don't get in our way. I can't make it more clear than that, Mr. Douglas."

"Guess not. Thanks." And, he turned and left. He walked back to his van and got in, mentally patting himself on the back. "That took some balls, Allen, my boy!" But, he was still not where he wanted to be in this matter.

******

Allie parked the newly acquired pickup in the back-parking lot of her building and entered through the rear. She walked up to the third floor. It was an old rooming house, but not bad. Just no elevator. She checked the refrigerator and there was nothing that interested her. The pain was beginning to set in seriously. She took four extra strength pain relievers and hoped they would help. Allie stripped and turned before the bathroom mirror to check her damage. Mainly bruising. What hurt was inside and she knew it was going to hurt more very soon. A hell of a lot more, so she took a long drag on the Bourbon bottle that had been sitting on the kitchen counter and went to bed.

As she lay there, she thought about the final two on her agenda. Leticia Foreman had proven the most contentious of all. Allie would have to have something special to pay her back. And, there was one more after Leticia. She had already located her. This one was a bit different than the others here in Florida. But, she knew that, physically, she would have to take a week off, maybe more.

CHAPTER 10

Sara went into the office on Sunday. She thought she would start some of the things that she had asked Maura to do Monday. After all, the detectives had had to do everything prior to the recent arrival of the crime analyst. She sent an email to George Abernathy's successor at the GBI to see if he could initiate a query about an attractive mid-thirties female cop leaving or getting fired somewhere in Georgia in the past ten years. Except for the botch-up in Naples, the murders had been almost professional in nature...like an intelligence operative or professional assassin. Or, maybe Allie had an accomplice...like Allen Douglas. If so, what was the connection between the two?

She sent the email to the GBI agent then fiddled with how to do such a specific query to VICAP and gave up. Murderers that clean and position their victims, murderers who used specific or unusual weapons, murderers who left all victims in dumpsters—these were things that were easier to search than a specific description of one who had also been a cop. Sara feared that most departments did not report their bad personnel to the FBI when there was nothing to report but that they had picked the wrong people to whom to give a badge and a gun.

Sara then gave thought to requesting help from one the

Bureau's Behavioral Assessment Units. That might mean losing the case to the feds. That would not usually worry her, but Sheriff MacNab had an election coming up in a few months and this was big news. Having his office solve it without federal or state assistance would help reinforce his successes as Sheriff of Osprey County. He had hired her directly into a detective position instead of putting her on the street as a deputy first. Sure, she had been a federal agent, but he still helped her, and she owed him.

Sara reviewed case files for several open cases; she had closed the burglaries and the alleged rape, but still had a garden variety of other crimes assigned. She had attached a post-it note to one file to call a source. The case was a drive-by shooting at one of the counties' few problematic housing projects. She blamed government for most of that, believing that jobs eliminated the vicious cycle of poverty better than anything. People were people, no matter their color or preference, and very few were intrinsically bad. They often did what they had to do. But, then, she thought of Allie. She was probably intrinsically bad.

******

Allie was thinking of her at the same time. She had picked up a vacationing neighbor's papers from outside his apartment door to find out what the cops knew about her. The Ft. Myers-based paper did not have the details about her that she suspected the Tampa one would. But, it did have some material about the detective working her case. It also mentioned the medical examiner, who seemed to be wherever the detective was. She would look into that. Allie had found that killing a cop was much easier than she thought. Maybe she would have some fun with these two.

She fired up her laptop and was surprised to see the lack of operational security, or OPSEC, that this Sara Nichols had. For $29.95 on the dead Mercedes woman's credit card, she found Nichol's address. Allie was a blade person and had tossed the dead cop's gun to the punks in the 'hood. It was going to be hard to take out the detective unless it was close and personal. And, she remembered she was a tall, athletic woman who could probably more than hold her own in a fight. That left the doctor, assuming there was something there to leverage.

Allie had been right about the pain. It was horrendous, even to someone of her constitution and will. She needed something much stronger than the extra strength pain relievers taken at multiples of their recommended dosage. But, where was she going to get it? She had seen the damage mentally that Oxy wrought. Maybe cruise and buy two. Two and never again anymore. She was tough enough to do that. Two was her magic number now. She had two adversaries: Leticia and the doctor, ne medical examiner. She had two remaining victims. One had been more trouble than all the rest put together. That redhead bitch with the killer heavy purse. She may meet her end a different way. Something less artistic than her first victims' razor. Allie had some ideas, but was still working on that.

She put on baggy jeans and a disreputable pullover. Her long blonde hair in a bun, she clamped a ball cap on her head. Over-sized aviator glasses completed her disguise. She got in the truck with her notes and some of the Mercedes bitch's cash.

First, she headed for the worst area she could find. She saw the mirror images of the guys from whom she had gotten the truck in trade for the stolen Mercedes.

"You got Oxy or a painkiller?"

"You a damn cop?"

"Nope." She pulled up her shirt, showing bare breasts. "No wire, see?"

"Twenty-five dollars each. Then get off my street."

She gave him the fifty in simultaneous swap for the pills. She hoped they were real as she powered off, the street kings scanning to see if there were police vehicles closing in. There were not.

Allie popped a pill and swallowed it with a gulp of water from a bottle from her refrigerator. She did a couple of right turns and checked her mirror. It did not appear that anyone had picked up a tail on her.

Her next stop was the address for the detective's house. It was a typical medium-priced Florida stucco ranch. Yard was neat, but not lovingly manicured. No vehicles apparent. She drove past at normal highway speeds. Slowing down would have been too obvious.

Then, she headed south. An hour later, she pulled into the marina where she had trailed Leticia Forman and the damn chase had begun. Pulling the truck in between two larger trucks, she slipped her pants off and a tiny bikini bottom on. It was followed by a string top, the triangles of cloth of which barely covered her aureoles. She untied her hair and shook it out, long and glossy. The ball cap was replaced with a big straw hat. Sunglasses and heeled sandals completed her ensemble. She reached under the seat, slipped the folded pearl-handled razor into the front of her bikini bottom and got out, a beach bag in hand.

Allie had seen the Audi parked in the lot when she pulled in. Either Leticia Forman was here working on her boat or was out on the water and would return before dark, she opined.

She decided to take a walk along the docks and see.

Leticia was on her boat, wearing a swimsuit bottom and a grubby tee-shirt as she pressure- washed the decks to remove fish blood, scales and sand from the tournament. Careful, she had a .380 Walther on the top of the console, covered with a cap. She loved the Bondish implications of it. She noticed a gorgeous woman walking down the dock. Okay, she could not see if the face was gorgeous, but the bathing suit was borderline legal in public and breasts were giggling and struggling to say within their tiny triangular cloth restraints. "Damn," she thought.

As the almost naked woman almost reached her boat, she set down a beach bag and turned, bending over to retrieve something. In so doing, she flashed Leticia a perfect ass and view of what lay a bit south. Leticia caught her breath.

Allie caught something else; it was a Molotov cocktail. She lit it with a Bic and tossed it at the redhead.

Leticia jumped aside as the bottle broke on the deck of her beautiful Mako center console, flames spreading everywhere as the fuel inside burned.

She could not get to the Walther, so she ran around the large console that held a portable potty inside and got the fire extinguisher. She was going to spray the almost-nude blonde, then her boat.

But, the blonde was already retreating at a good speed, sure that the tough Leticia was now burning up. Leticia wanted to run after her and kill her with her bare hands. But, she had to save her beloved boat. Just as taught in the Coast Guard Auxiliary boating safety course, she swept the flow from the fire extinguisher back and forth at the base of the flames. A cry went up—marina fires spread fast and sink valuable craft. Several charter captains and the dock master came to her aid with more fire extinguishers. The flame was knocked down within several minutes. It appeared, other than soot, there was little damage. The fire had flashed upon itself more than the fiberglass deck and sides. Leticia picked up her smartphone and dialed 911. She requested that Detective Nichols be apprised. Though the fire was out, the dock master had pulled the fire alarm at the "whoosh" flame-up of the bomb and fire apparatus was en route.

A dock hand a hundred feet away had seen Allie toss the firebomb and ran towards the blonde as she fled the scene. As he approached her, she spun a hundred eighty degrees and caught him in the center of the chest with her heel. The roundhouse karate kick sent him off the dock and into the water. A second man, working on a nearby boat saw this and jumped to the dock, blocking Allie. Her bikini bottom was so small that the razor handle stuck out several inches above the waistband, had there been one. She drew the razor and flipped it open and slashed. He saw it coming and jumped back, getting only his shirt opened by the edge of the square blade. As he was off-balance, Allie moved in and reared back on her left leg and gave him more of a powerful push than kick with her left. He also went into the water, but not as lucky as the dock hand, hit his head on the deck of his own boat first and entered the saltwater of the harbor unconscious.

Allie walked on, hurriedly, but not running. She knew that anyone who had not seen her throw the Molotov, or down the two men, would only focus—male or female—on her exposed and lovely anatomy. She smiled pleasantly as she walked back to her truck and departed the scene. Just like when she left Tampa General, she had to skirt responding fire trucks as she pulled away.

******

Sara was leaving the office as she got the radio call from the marina. She aimed the Charger towards the marina and accelerated. She called Leticia from her cell.

"Hey, it's Sara. I'm on the way. What happened?"

"She came back, looking like a million dollars and threw a firebomb at me. I ducked it and a couple of us got the fire out before it did much damage. She got away after knocking two guys in the water. One may be serious."

"Okay, hang tight. I will be there in ten minutes or less."

"I will. I had my .380, but the flames were between it and me. I would have shot the bitch, Sara. I swear I would have!"

"Well, it would have solved the case, kind of. But, it's not something you would like to live with the rest of your life."

"Oh, I could deal with that just fine. Believe me!"

Sara grinned to herself. This one has moxie. She probably could live with it just fine. Then, she concentrated on dodging traffic and getting on-scene quickly.

Sara marked on scene. One deputy, Shawna Gilson, had already begun questioning witnesses as paramedics attempted to resuscitate the man who had hit his head upon going into the water. They got a pulse and stabilized him to transport. No twelfth victim yet.

She got everyone to line up outside the dock master's office and started interviewing Leticia.

"Sara, I saw this woman coming towards me and she had the tiniest bikini I have ever seen on a perfect body. I was getting turned on just watching her walk towards me. Just before she got to my boat, she turned away and bent over. Oh, my God! Then, she turned and quickly threw a firebomb into the Mako. I dodged it as it hit, broke at flames instantly spread on the area behind the console. She took off, though not running. I could not reach the gun, so I decided to save the boat. Because of some quick help, I mainly have a shitload of soot to clean up, instead of a new boat to buy."

As Sara interviewed other witnesses, each corroborated the other by stating that the beautiful woman was almost naked and used professionally perfect martial arts kicks to effortlessly move the two men out of her way and into the water. Not that it really mattered in view of the other charges Allie faced, but two more battery charges would be levied in Osprey County.

It was past five by the time the interviews were over. Sara walked back down to the Mako to check on Leticia.

"Nothing really new, except that her movements seemed to have formal training. We have been toying with the idea she might have been military or a cop. Kills without breaking a sweat, including an experienced cop, leaves no evidence, picks up vehicles with apparent ease."

"Well, I have about had enough of this shit, Sara. I had a hard early life, caught a break and worked my ass off bettering myself. I have the perfect life. Maybe one day, I will want a wife to share it with, but now I don't."

"I feel the same way, Leticia."

"You hungry?" Leticia asked.

"Starving. No lunch. Again. I have tentative plans with Lynn Goddard, the medical examiner and wanted to check on Sally Henson, who was the lover of the first Florida victim. How about if I see if we can put together a four-girl dinner? I think you'd like the other two."

"Sure! I have a sundress hanging in the car. Just picked it up at the cleaners and forgot to take it in to the house. Let me take a quick shower here at the marina while you make the calls."

"Okay, but I will check the shower room first!"

"No argument there! I don't want to get my Walther .380 wet and have it rust."

Leticia retrieved the Walther PPK and put it in a canvas tote, along with her laptop and phone. They two walked to the shower room. It appeared no one was there. While Leticia undressed, Sara checked the four shower stalls to make sure they were empty. She turned one on to allow the heated water to get to it. As she turned, she saw the nude redhead walk in, carrying a towel and squeeze bottle of moisturizing body wash.

She smiled at Sara. "Need a shower? I have a whole bottle of wash. Can use it as shampoo, too."

Sara was tempted. But, she replied. "Not tonight. But, soon sounds fun. Rain check?"

Leticia caressed Sara's cheek on the way by and said, "Rain check given."

Sara stood outside for a second savoring what she had just seen, then placed two calls successfully. Both Lynn and Sally were available and interested. They agreed that the marina from which Sara was calling and Leticia was showering had the most central good waterfront to everyone's current location.

Forty minutes later, three beautiful women in sundresses were seated by the railing overlooking the water. One beautiful woman who had changed into a non-sheriff's logo golf shirt and had switched her holstered Sig for a back-up in an ankle holster hidden by the cuff of the same slacks she had arrived in, sat with them. They were sharing a large pitcher of sangria and dipping taco chips into some very spicy fruit salsa.

"Sally," Leticia began, "do you like boats and fishing?"

"I do! I am not very good at fishing, but used to go with my grandfather when I was a girl. He had something called a johnboat and we would launch it in the Upper Manatee River and catch all sorts of stuff."

"Well, I can always use a crew for my tournaments. Maybe this group should be my next crew! Lynn, do you boat or fish?"

"I SUP and kayak. I went to the Keys once with Sara and we fished with her brother, who's a professional fishing guide. We caught dolphin and grouper. Boy, did we eat well!"

"Dolphin?" Sally asked, with a worried look on her face.

Leticia jumped in. "She is talking about the dolphin fish, honey. Not the porpoises. Don't worry. She didn't eat Flipper."

"Who?" Sally asked, showing her youth and innocence...at least about sea life and early television series.

"Just an old TV show starring a porpoise. Not to worry," Leticia said.

Sally gave her an appreciative look and seemed to communicate something that both Sara and Lynn picked up on, but did not acknowledge.

After dinner, Sara warned the three to keep alert. Everyone but Sally admitted to being armed, though that Sara carried was a given. Sally looked left out and Leticia suggested that she may want to spend the night at her house since a very violent Allie was out and about. Sara agreed with the efficacy of that, and Sally followed Leticia home. And, Lynn followed Sara home.

And, Allie followed Lynn to Sara's home and waited patiently, albeit painfully.

******

Sara put her backup pistol on the table beside the pool and next to the towels. She stepped in the shallow end of the pool, where a similarly unadorned medical examiner was floating on a pool float, a plastic wine stem in the holder on its arm rest.

"This Allie is like a chameleon. She changes her appearance as she wants, seems to be impervious to death, shows up wherever. It is starting to make me nervous, Sara."

"Me, too, honey."

"I know the solution."

"What's that?"

"Unabated, wild and dirty sex."

"Starting when?"

"Right now."

"You're on."

They cut the pool time short and went into the house. Allie patiently waited from a half block away.

Three hours later, a drained, smiling Lynn was walked out to her car. She left and Sara went into the house and climbed into bed with her two naked men, Gibbs and DiNozzo.

A pickup truck followed Lynn home. She did not notice it. As she hit the automatic opener for her garage, the pick-up's driver watched from the curb a hundred yards south and noted everything about the good doctor's townhouse community. No gate. No cameras. No patrol.

******

Dolly Woodson got in a little after twelve, parking her Bur-gundy Miata with its tan soft top. She was the manager at a higher tier chain restaurant with a waterfront location and seemed to spend more time at work than at home. Despite feeling haggard, the thirty-six-year old looked great. She had long black hair, blue eyes and curves in all the right places. She was medium height. Dolly did not work out per se. She just worked, moving for fourteen hour shifts almost without pause.

She and her lover, a newspaper editor, were consid-ering moving in with each other. Their big problem was not commitment, it was whose house to keep and whose to get rid of. Both loved their homes and had put sweat equity and differing décor into them. Dolly liked classic Queen Anne furnishings; the editor ran more towards modern. A combination of Queen Anne and Victorian or American Primitive…maybe. Queen Anne and modern… not so much. They agreed that the term "eclectic" could only be bent so far. While Dolly did not have the degree the editor had, she suspected that she had a higher IQ and knew she was ranked higher on the stubborn meter. Hence, they were at an impasse that did not worry either. The relationship was fairly strong and did not yet require constant companionship. Maybe, it never would. And, thought Dolly, if the editor found another beauty who liked modern furniture, *C'est la vie*!

Dolly considered a pet instead of a spouse. Her lifestyle did not allow a dog, so a cat or goldfish were the likely answer. She went into the kitchen and poured a glass of a blended wine she had discovered while checking wine lists at the restaurant. It had overtones of fruit and chocolate without the attendant calories of those foods. She kicked off her shoes and sat in the den. She turned on the Bose and sipped the wine. Soon, she was asleep. In the middle of the night, she would awaken, drag to the bedroom, leave her clothes in a pile on the floor and collapse upon the bed. She did not have to go in tomorrow until eleven AM and planned to sleep as long as she could and as deeply.

As she slept, a pickup truck sat parked several doors down from her townhouse condominium. Its driver also tired and in a great deal of pain that a fake Oxycontin did not help. The driver considered going back to where she had gotten the two pills and introducing the seller to a pearl-handled razor. Allie could be quite vindictive and took pride in it.

CHAPTER 11

Earlier that night, or more properly that morning, Joseph "Big" Taylor and his friend Bobby Ruskin decided it was time to take the new Mercedes for a cruise. They left the product at home, taking only the Glock the crazy woman had given them.

The car was full of fuel and looked like it had just been detailed, which it actually had. They drove out from behind the aunt's house where "Big" lived and proceeded down the street that led out of the projects toward Tampa's famed Ybor City and a club they liked.

As they cruised down East 7th Avenue in Ybor, a Tampa cop in his patrol car wondered how two teens could afford to drive an almost hundred thousand dollar set of wheels. His partner called it in and the tags came back to the carjacking that followed the murder of one of their brothers in blue. They called for backup. The two officers could see the driver and passenger starting to get nervous. The did not want to make a felony stop on a main drag through a historic part of Tampa, still busy on a weekend clubbing night. But, under the circumstances surrounding the vehicle, they had no other option. They lit up the Mercedes. Luckily, their backup unit pulled around a corner and blocked the German sedan.

The officers from the blocking cruiser moved to the passenger side of their vehicle and the officers from the stopping cruiser moved to the driver side of theirs, avoiding a cross-fire situation if things got hot.

The officer who had been driving squatted behind his door, mic in hand. His partner had his patrol rifle aimed at the Mercedes.

"Driver in the Mercedes, this is the Tampa Police. Turn off your engine. Put the windows down and drop the keys outside. Do it now!"

The driver, to the surprise of the officers, complied.

"Now, driver first. Get out of the car with your hands above your head."

The three men and one woman in uniform knew this was where, if the driver was going to be stupid, it would manifest itself.

And, it did. "Big" rolled out of the car and snapped a shot at the officers. A pedestrian fifty yards down the sidewalk caught the round in the chest.

The officer with the M-4 patrol rifle fired two fast shots, killing "Big" instantly. Bobby Ruskin stuck both hands out of the passenger window and stayed there until the two officers in front dragged him through the open car window and placed him unceremoniously face down on the sidewalk.

The first two officers, after placing a "shots fired" call, moved carefully in on the fallen "Big." The widening pool of blood suggested that the wound was serious. The driver turned him over while the officer with the rifle covered him. "Big's" eyes were open, but unfocused. The officer kicked the Glock on the street out of the man's reach out of procedure, not current need. He knew that the two fifty-five grain bullets that had hit the man in the heart a half an inch apart at thirty-two hundred feet per second had had the hydrostatic effect of exploding his heart. "Big" was deceased but did not yet realize it. Within seconds, he might. Or, he might just succumb without another thought.

The response was large and the investigation, though a "clean" shoot, was long. The first thing that was done after the body had been declared DOA and covered, was the serial number was carefully noted from the gun, without lessening its evidentiary status. It was done the old way; a pen was stuck in the barrel, the serial number written down, and the loaded gun placed in an evidence bag with "loaded" noted in heavy Sharpie letters. In a police shooting, everything had to be examined fairly. The gun would be unloaded later under conditions that would not smudge any fingerprints on it.

A quick check indicated that it was the gun stolen by Allie from the police officer she had killed.

By four in the morning, detectives had Bobby singing. He told them about the crazy woman and described the pickup truck. Sometimes the system worked. It did this time, and a Tampa detective left a voicemail for Detective Sara Nichols at her desk by six thirty Monday morning. She arrived at the office at six forty-five and now had a description of the latest vehicle Allie was driving. Respecting Maura's graphic skills above her own, she waited for the analyst to arrive to prepare a statewide BOLO, adding the truck to the one already extant on Allie.

Sara drove to the marina with her case notes and re-interviewed everyone she could find there from the firebomb incident. None had seen the truck. But, that did not mean it had not been there. Unless someone saw the woman in the tiny bikini get into or out of it, there would be no reason to notice a nondescript truck. Twenty-one percent of all vehicles on the road in America are pickups, so it would not stand out, especially in a largely rural Florida county.

Sara took copies of the BOLO to FedEx, UPS, the US

Postal Service, county agencies, the transit system, taxi companies, and the local Florida Department of Transportation office. She wanted as many eyes on the road as possible to be looking for her killer. This may be the boost her case needed.

******

Dolly came home and began to prepare for a date with the editor. She had but an hour and stripped for her bath. She heard the doorbell. The editor had a key, so she hastily put on a terry cloth robe and peered out of the peephole.

She saw a very lovely woman of approximately her age. She had a business suit on and carried a briefcase. Leaving the chain intact, she cracked the door and said, "Yes?"

"Agent Simms, IRS. I need to visit with you a few minutes over some irregularities with your last return."

"I really can't do this now. Can't you schedule another time? I have a CPA; she should be present. All I do is sign the returns and write or cash the checks."

With that, Allie threw her hundred forty pounds against the door. The chain came out of the wall, held only be short screws, and the door hit Dolly in the face, knocking her down. Allie glanced backwards, reasonably sure that no one had seen what she did and stepped in, closing the door and locking it. Dolly tried to get to her feet and Allie kicked her in the side of the face. She went down immediately and did not get back up.

Allie reached into the open top briefcase and withdrew white cotton gloves and put them on. She smudged the door handle she had touched.

Allie picked up the unconscious Dolly Woodson and carried her into what appeared to be the master bedroom. She ripped the robe off and spread-eagled her on the king-sized bed. Before she could gain consciousness, Allie slid the pearl-handled razor along her throat and warm blood soiled the comforter. Dolly died with a gurgle and a convulsive jerk of her body. And, now there was only one. That damned strawberry blonde. And, maybe the tall female cop for good measure. Both seemed tough, but she was trained for it and had the element of surprise on her side.

Allie quickly stripped off the suit jacket and skirt and removed a cover-up from the briefcase. She put the suit inside and the cover-up on along with a ball cap and sunglasses from the briefcase. She picked up a beach towel from Dolly's bathroom and draped it over her arm as she slipped out of the sliding glass doors. Once outside, she closed the door and removed the gloves. She put them in the briefcase and draped the beach towel over it. With the cap hiding her hair color and sunglasses on, a bikini and slight cover-up, she looked enough like Dolly to pass from a distance. She walked to the pool, nodded at a few people who nodded back without enthusiasm, and put the towel down on a chaise. She took the briefcase and walked into the clubhouse. In the dressing room, she put the suit back on and walked out the front door to where her truck was parked in the shade of a tree. She drove off satisfied with what she considered a job well done.

******

William Patrick Grayson pulled his entry-level BMW 100 series to the curb outside Dolly's house. He was her boyfriend, the editor whose taste in décor conflicted with Dolly's. He saw her Miata out front and let himself in.

"Lucy, I'm home," he sang out in his best Ricky Ricardo voice. Dolly did not reply, so William went into the bedroom where he saw the gruesome sight posed for him. He picked up the phone and dialed 911 and reported the obvious murder. He then threw up all over his shoes and the cuffs of his suit pants. William sat on the side of the bed next to her bare feet and rocked back and forth sobbing.

The first deputy on scene recognized the *modus ope-randi* and requested Sara be among the other responders.

Sara responded from the office and arrived quickly. No question about the murder or the suspect. This was differ-ent from the other Florida murders…it was a male lover left in anguish, not a female. The only similarities were the approximate age and the slit throat. Unless it was found that Dolly was bi, this would represent a change in targets, perhaps a broadening of the target base. Sara hoped that was not the case. Though the body was staged nude, the robe laying in a pile in the floor beside the bed suggested that she may have had it on. A tear was present in a location that suggested it had been ripped off. The corpse of Dolly Woodson had several bruises that indicated she had been attacked and had probably lost some capacity to defend herself before being slashed. Again, no DNA was obvious under Dolly's manicure. The amount of blood on the bed was conclusive proof that she had been killed there.

Lynn arrived and determined that the time of death had been less than an hour ago. The newspaper editor had not seen anyone suspicious when he arrived.

Sara left the photographing of the crime scene to her CSI team. She walked around the apartment. She liked the décor and picked up a few decorating ideas for her own place.

She saw that the back sliding door was not locked. All evidence and a quick interview of the boyfriend had indi-cated a date night. So, why was the back of the apartment insecure? Sara went back to the living room and asked Wil-liam Patrick Grayson if Dolly usually left doors insecure.

"No, not at all. She was very security conscious."

"Mr. Grayson, did you hear anyone leave or any suspi-cious noises when you came in?"

"No."

Sara knew that, in view of Lynn's time of death determination, he must have come in just after the murder had occurred. It was probable, in view of that and the unlocked slider, that Allie had left by the rear slider. Sara walked out and looked around. There was a children's playground to the right. To the left, she saw a sidewalk leading to a club house. She saw the privacy fence of a large swimming pool and a tennis court beyond. Sara walked along the sidewalk to the pool.

"Hi, folks. I am Detective Sara Nichols, with the Osprey Sheriff's Office. Did any of you see a taller woman in her thirties come through this way in the past hour?"

"Yeah," and older man with a leathery suntan replied. "she had on a bathing suit and left her towel on the chair by where you are standing. A looker she was, too."

"Where did she go, sir?" Sara asked.

"Took a briefcase looking thing and walked into the club house. Figured she needed the Wi-Fi or had to pee. Never came back out."

"Thanks," Sara said as she walked through the door to the locker rooms and exercise rooms, hand near the butt of her gun. The exercise room and women's locker room were empty. She searched the men's locker and frightened a guy in the shower. She was not about to announce her police presence to a murder suspect just to preserve privacy.

There were several people in a lounge area, availing themselves of the free Wi-Fi.

"May I have your attention? I am Detective Nichols. Have any of you been here for the past forty-five minutes or hour? Yes? Excellent, Ma'am. Did you happen to see anyone walk through this area from the locker room?"

"I saw a tallish woman about a half hour or so ago. She was wearing a business suit, but her sandals didn't match. Too casual. What's going on?"

"There was a homicide in the complex in the last hour. The person may be the suspect. Please tell me what she looked like, as best as you can."

"She had blonde hair in a bun and sunglasses on, even though she was inside. Her suit was either tan or light gray...I don't remember. The sandals were pink. They clashed."

"That helps. Did any of you happen to see her vehicle?"

No one responded.

"Did anyone happen to notice a black Nissan Frontier pickup—maybe five years old—parked outside?"

Again, no luck. Sara thanked everyone and went back to her car and got evidence tape and, returning to the women's restroom, cordoned it off for her CSI team. Finding Allie's prints—once she was captured and printed—would at least corroborate that she was in the complex at the time of the murder.

Once more, she returned to the apartment and resumed interviewing the boyfriend about Dolly's background, job location, and whether she had any enemies. The latter was more procedural than necessary. Sara knew who Dolly's enemy had been. Just not why. When she pressed Grayson as to whether Dolly had ever expressed any bisexual tendencies, he became irate. She let him blow off steam and quietly told him that every other person in this case who had been killed like this was a lesbian. Except, apparently for Dolly. And that presented a significant difference that needed to be understood to solve the case. He calmed down and admitted that, as a newspaper editor, he had followed the case in the articles he had approved and was aware of that. He was apologetic and broke down again. Sara escorted him out of the crime scene and to his car, advising him to go home and rest, all the time looking at him and thanking God that she was a lesbian. She was aware that he had either written or approved an article suggesting that she had used excessive force taking down the wife-beater in the park. Damn anti-cop wimp, she concluded as she smiled and closed his car door. She wished she could close it on his foot.

The only interesting thing that came out of the interview was that Dolly had grown up in Georgia and was vague, even to an "almost-fiancé," as he described himself, about her family and early life. Possibly a tie-in to the original Georgia murders, Sara thought to herself.

She had Dolly's purse and some financial and historical paperwork she had picked up at the apartment. Maybe, just maybe that would help Maura and her to track Dolly back to the Georgia days and figure out what the tie-in was.

******

Allie had accomplished all but one of her long-term goals with the murder of Dolly Woodson. She still had Leticia Foreman on her agenda. A news article had discussed the attack at the marina and the person Allie had thought was dead was interviewed. That bitch was proving herself a royal pain. She should have been much easier to kill. "Well," she thought, "her day will come and really damn soon!"

She almost wished that she had a gun. Clearly, she could get one, but she liked the elegance of a blade. Allie had resorted to an IED for the boat attack. She may have to go that route again with the Forman bitch. She was big and fairly fit and not afraid to fight. Allie wanted to finish her tasks and move on to a quieter life somewhere outside of Florida, but with similar weather. She did not have vast sums of money to fund moving to Mexico or Costa Rica, so she needed to give that problem some thought. However, she could not focus on anything but her plan. And now, she had added the tall, problematic detective to the plan. But, she had already figured out how to lure her into an ambush. Allie smiled to herself.

Good procedures suggested that she replace the truck with a different vehicle. She had not had cops buzzing all around like this before. She was thinking a bike this time to mix things—and people—up. She would get one tonight. That should not be a problem.

She headed back to her apartment and parked the truck around back where it was not obvious to anyone. Four pain-killers and a full glass of bourbon and she stripped and laid across the bed. Allie knew that her internal clock would wake her a bit after dark…if the pain did not wake her first.

******

Leticia worked late that night, preparing the paperwork for the loans for four real estate closings. The economy nationally might not be great, but her business with union pensioners moving to Florida was booming. These were people who could pay cash for their final home but chose to get a loan and invest the money to pay off the loan. Also, she had prior clients who were getting along in age and had no beneficiaries and she made them reverse mortgages. She was kind and patient and only offered options she sincerely thought were best for her clients. And, the word of that spread with little additional effort from her. Realtors constantly referred clients to her, sometimes even if they had an in-house mortgage affiliate.

Leticia was a one broker and one mortgage assistant shop. She was thinking seriously about adding another broker so she could have time to enjoy life instead of working all the time.

She had attended a self-improvement seminar recently and had remembered the context of a quote by the Dalai Lama which said something like the thing that surprised him the most about humanity was man himself, who sacrifices his health to make money, sacrifices money to recuperate his health and is so anxious about the future he does not enjoy the present. She knew that could have been said of her. She was going to make a conscious effort to change.

Leticia pressed the opener on her garage and pulled in. She did not see Allie slip in behind her and never saw the blow that knocked her unconscious. Allie lifted her back into her car and restarted the engine. She buckled Leticia in and hooked her hands to the steering wheel with wire ties. Duct tape held a garden hose to the Audi's exhaust and the pressure of the electric window held it aimed inside the vehicle. Allie knew a blade would have given her more pleasure, but this totally different M.O. would baffle the detective. She took the door remote from the sun visor and slipped out of the garage into the dark. She pressed the remote and the door closed. She suspected that, within a minute or two the automatic light would go off, leaving Leticia, once she awakened in stark panic. It served her right.

Allie had made an error this time; she had not noticed that the connecting door from the garage was ajar, bypassed from the security alarm. It did not take long for carbon monoxide to fill the one-car garage and seep into the main residence. The utility room adjacent to the garage was only large enough to hold a stacked washer and dryer and connected to the kitchen via a short hall. That hall had a built-in carbon dioxide detector that went off and reported to the alarm company, which immediately dispatched Osprey County Fire Rescue. Sara had the residence's address on an alert status with 911 calls for service and was immediately notified at home. She jumped in the Charger and ran at top speed to Leticia's.

She arrived just as paramedics were carrying an unconscious Leticia out to the driveway, oxygen attached. Sara was relieved to see they were not giving CPR or readying the defibrillator.

She stayed back and let the experts ply their trade until she was sure that Leticia was not in danger. Then, she walked into the garage and looked around. She saw a length of dowel protruding from beneath the Audi. Using nitrile gloves, she retrieved it and noted that it did not have blood or hair, but she was sure it was what was used to render Leticia unconscious. She went out and told the paramedics to check the back of her head once they had her breathing on her own. One immediately slipped her hand behind Leticia's head and nodded.

"Yep. There's a goose egg there. No blood, just a knot," she reported. "We should transport her and have the docs take an X-ray and make sure the carbon monoxide did not do any long-term harm. You may want to interview her in the hospital once all that is done, Sara."

"Absolutely. I will follow you."

The transport was not Code-3, just a quick ride to the ER. A team was waiting and Leticia was rushed in on a gurney and taken to an examination room in the ER. Sara got a cup of coffee from the nurse's station and sat in the waiting room. She was frustrated and the best thing she could come up with was "that's why they call it a waiting room." That moment of brilliance did not give her a whit's satisfaction, so Sara sat without thinking for almost a millisecond and then gave up and began to be frustrated again about why she had not caught this elusive chameleon.

******

Dr. Lynn Goddard pulled her SUV into her garage and pressed the remote to close the garage door. She was tired; it had been a busy day at the medical examiner's office, more from paperwork and politics than anything else. But, she did not complain. If she were in private practice, her work schedule would be far worse and far less interesting.

She walked in the house and kicked off her shoes. She then worked the bra out from beneath her blouse and felt comfort top and bottom. Style sucked, she mouthed silently to herself.

That was the last thing she remembered as Allie hit her behind the neck with a karate chop and the lights went out. When she awakened shortly thereafter, she was trussed with plastic wire ties and unable to speak through the duct tape over her mouth.

Allie had gotten Lynn's cell phone from her purse.

"Put in the code," she said, punctuating the order with a vicious kick to the shins. Allie watched and memorized the PIN as she entered it.

Lynn complied. Allie looked through the phone and found the voicemail. She would put in the message she had planned once they were away and had a head start on Detective Nichols. Now that she had finished Leticia after a few false starts, the last one on her revised list was Nichols. Since she was armed and trained, Allie could not rely totally on her razor, so she had added a few more toys to her toy box.

It was dark when they went out Lynn's back gate and circled to a parking lot a block from her residence. A beat-up SUV was waiting. It had a canoe atop that was worth more than the truck. The Mad River Kevlar canoe was fast and a good trekker. Just what Allie had in mind. Besides, the hippie-looking canoeist would not be needing it anymore. He would not be needing anything anymore. And, with his camping gear, he had graciously though unintentionally supplied Allie with most of what she needed for this last project before blowing town.

Allie drove to the park where Sara had arrested the wife-beater. She took the canoe off the carrier on the rusted-out SUV and set paddles and her other equipment in it.

She dragged it to the edge of the water at the put-in, then got Lynn out of the SUV and led her to the canoe.

"Sit in it. Here's the deal. I have nothing against you. You are chattel. You can live if you behave and your friend Nichols does what I ask. Or, you can die. I guess you know I have killed a lot of people. One more won't make me swing any higher. I will tie you to the seat of the canoe. That means you better not turn it over. You will drown and I won't help you. I will cut the ones off your wrists to that you can paddle from the front. Try anything stupid and you will die quickly, but horribly. You understand?"

Lynn nodded, more angered than scared. The fear would likely come later, she knew. This one was a psycho. It did not take her medical degree to diagnose that.

Allie positioned Lynn and the canoe just slightly to the side of the ramp, which was used for power boat launching. She got in the old SUV and revved it. She tied the accelerator down, with the truck pointed at the ramp, threw it in gear and jumped out. The SUV roared down the ramp into the water and floated for a second or two before it unceremoniously sank, amid hissing and bubbles. Not only would it take the truck out of the picture, it would block the ramp from police boat or game warden launches.

Allie entered the memorized PIN into Lynn's phone and recorded a new voicemail greeting. She then handed Lynn a paddle and demanded that she dig in and paddle because they had miles to go in the dark.

CHAPTER 12

Sara arrived at her house around eight o'clock and fed Gibbs and DiNozzo. She looked around for something for dinner and settled on an eggplant parmesan prepared dish from her freezer. She opened a bottle of Pinot Grigio and sat down to eat, still agitating about the case. She had a deputy watching Leticia and had warned him about what happened to the last police officer who had watched someone related to this case. She took some solace in the fact that, unless Allie was hiding nearby and observing at Leticia's home, she probably thought that Leticia was dead.

Around nine, she picked up her phone and called Lynn. The phone rang and rang, until it went into voicemail and Sara's heart almost stopped when she heard what she realized immediately was Allie's voice.

"If you are not Detective Nichols, get this message to her verbatim. If you are, bitch, listen closely. I have Dr. Goddard. If you want to ever see her alive, you have to do two things. One, do not call your department, the state or the FBI. If you do, I promise that she will die. First plane, first patrol boat, bang! Second, get a canoe or kayak and go to where you arrested the wife-beater. Paddle south on the Blueway for five miles. Wear a light on your head, so I will know it's you. No surveillance planes or helos, no

FLIR or other fancy shit. Don't bring a gun. When I see you, I will flash a light and you will beach your boat where you saw the light. When I am sure you are alone and no threat, I will make myself known. I have no argument with the doctor, but I will kill her without hesitation if you provoke me. Got that?" No more words were spoken. Sara got a notebook and replayed the recording, taking notes to make sure nothing was missed. She heard seabird noises and some wind. That signaled that the recording must have been made near the water, probably at the launch. Allie probably timed it that way to get a good head start and be ready in ambush.

Sara knew the procedures. Call out the cavalry on one like this. Especially the Feds. She knew that was what she was supposed to do. But, this was Lynn's life. She thought a small surgical operation may work. She had been trained for such ops in the NCIS. She backed out the Jeep and put the kayak on top. It was a fourteen-foot sea kayak and had a rudder. That meant it was fast and tracked in a straight line, even in tidal waters like she would be facing tonight.

Sara dressed in cargo shorts over her bikini bottom and a fishing shirt with multiple pockets over a sports bra.

She started carrying things out to the side of the Jeep. First, she got her patrol rifle out of the Charger. It was a semi-automatic .223 like the military carried. She added a survival "bug-out" bag with first aid, Mylar blanket, a tactical flashlight, cyalume light sticks, emergency rations and a fixed blade knife. She put a lensatic compass, headband flashlight, and her handheld police radio and a handheld VHF with Coast Guard channels within immediate reach in a canvas duffle. Sara added a couple of Nalgene bottles with cold water. She was as ready as she would ever be. She put the duffle in the Jeep and pulled out of the drive and drove south.

At the park, the entrance to which was luckily not chained, due to late-arriving boaters and paddlers, she unloaded the kayak and put the items from the duffle in a hatch. She put her backup pistol in a cargo pocket in her shorts and put the headband light on, with a cap over it, backwards to not obstruct the beam. A water bottle, energy bar, tactical flashlight, the rifle and two radios in waterproof bags went in the cockpit with her. She set off with more than a little apprehension.

She timed her pace from markers and began to slow at three miles. It would be a good trap to say five miles and ambush at three. Sara still did not have the headband light turned on. She paddled by occasionally turning on the tactical light with its blinding three hundred lumen beam to read markers, or by using its low setting to read her compass. She saw an island ahead and wondered if it was the one where Allie waited with Lynn. Thought Allie was a constant surprise, Sara doubted that she would have night vision glasses or NVGs. Instead of turning on the headlamp, she stayed several hundred yards offshore and circled the island. She quietly beached on the opposite side from the one where she suspected Allie would watch for her. She knew that Allie would have the times of the two voicemail calls on Lynn's phone, but still would not know when she actually left, or what her progress was. She thought the stealth and fact that Allie did not know her progress were in her favor.

Sara dialed Lynn's number and got the same voicemail. She knew that Allie would monitor the phone. She left a message: "Can you see me? I have the light on and have been paddling for an hour and a half. I have to be near you. Flash your light if you see me."

She took the rifle out of the cockpit of the beached kayak and began to circle the longer way around the island, coming in from the right, not the more expected offshore left. Sara would walk fifty feet and stop for several minutes, listening. It took her thirty minutes to circle the island and come within several hundred yards of where she estimated Allie to be waiting for her. Sara continually prayed that this was the right island. Otherwise, she could be wasting precious time and maybe Lynn's life at the hands of this psycho.

She had felt the wind pick up while paddling and had been glad for the rudder and the long waterline of the sea kayak. Now the wind was working both for and against her. It was somewhat masking her approach, though moving through sand was relatively quiet. It, however, impaired her ability to hear any noises that Allie or Lynn might make. Without those, Sara would not know where they were and might walk right in front of them and be mowed down.

The moon moved from behind a cloud, illuminating the beach. She looked for skid marks on the beach where a vessel, canoe or whatever, had been dragged up. She assumed canoe or tandem kayak, since it would be hard to control a prisoner in two separate kayaks.

It got brighter for a moment and Sara saw a drag line. She had to assume that Allie and Lynn would be directly inshore from it. They could have moved in either direction, but Sara had no way of knowing. She hit redial on her phone, turning away and cupping it in her hand to block the light signature.

She heard a phone ring fifty feet away, just to the left of where the drag line would have indicated. Mistake on Allie's part. She should have silenced the ringer. Sara moved quietly towards the sound of the ring. After ten steps, she heard a "whish" and felt an immediate burn in her left side.

"Shit!" she said to herself. It was either an arrow or a crossbow bolt. She hoped the former, since the latter was easier for most people to shoot accurately. And, that had been a good shot. She felt wetness rolling down her side, but knew it had grazed her and not penetrated. If it had penetrated, she would be well on the way to dead by now.

As trained at FLETC for the NCIS and later at the Sheriff's Academy refresher, Sara had immediately moved to the side and dropped in the sea grapes at the first shot of the crossbow. The heard the noise again and more felt than saw a bolt fly past at the approximate location she had been standing.

For all Sara knew, Lynn could be standing in front of or next to Allie, so returning fire was not an option until she had identified her target without question. She dropped down into a commando crawl position and began to silently and laboriously move towards where she thought the two would be. Her side was really beginning to burn, but she did not have the luxury of applying a Quik-Clot blood staunching pad, or even direct pressure. She had to get to Allie and neutralize her. She had hoped it would not come to this, but her op had moved to life or death now.

As an osprey called in its distinctive way, Sara used the bird sound to click the high lumen flashlight onto the clip below the forearm of the rifle. It was close enough to her support hand to turn it on without a major position change.

Sara saw a shadowy figure run out of the brush, dragging a canoe to the water. She could not fire as she could not do a positive identification. It would be good tactics for Allie to send Lynn out to draw fire, while using the sounds and flashes to send more crossbow bolts her way.

Sara saw another figure run out onto the sand and trip, as if her feet where hobbled. Sara turned on the rifle flash, her finger away from the trigger and three hundred lumens of brilliant light lit up the figure. It was Lynn!

She saw the other figure, now in the canoe forty feet from shore, turn and appear to aim. Sara raised the rifle and fired four times in quick succession. The target rolled and the canoe did also. Sara saw the canoe drift off. She scanned the water with the powerful light attached to her rifle and did not see a head or shoulders in the water. It appeared she had made a kill shot and Allie had sunk, to bloat and resurface later.

Sara called out, "Lynn! It's me! I am coming."

Lynn was still tied, hobbled and had duct tape over her mouth, which she was working, but emitting only unintelligible sounds.

Sara looked again towards the canoe and saw nothing. She sat the rifle down and pulled her knife. She cut the bindings and with a great deal of sympathy, jerked the duct tape off beautiful lips.

Lynn fell into Sara's arms.

"I cannot believe I was so dumb as to be caught and to be used as bait for that nutcase to try to kill you. I am so sorry, Sara!"

"You have nothing to apologize about! You are a victim. You didn't choose to be abducted. I was so worried about you. We have to get on the radio and call the Coast Guard. They can get a boat and helicopter here before anybody."

Sara pulled the VHF handheld radio out of her pocket and put out a distress call on channel sixteen. The Coast Guard answered, got the location and situation and had Sara switch to channel twenty-two alpha for more details. Sara gave the GPS position in latitude and longitude from the reading on the face of the radio, and requested a boat and helicopter be sent for a recovery search of Allie's body. Then, she made the call she dreaded. The one to her own agency, where she had broken every rule in the book by not notifying anyone. She could get fired for this or get demoted to being a detention deputy. Either way, it was probably a career ender. Dispatch rolled the county fire/rescue boat and the Sheriff's patrol boat and a Game and Wildlife Commission warden's boat to their location. She knew that the dispatcher would also alert the LT and the Chief Deputy. Maybe even the Sheriff. Whatever hell may come her way, Lynn was safe. That was all that really mattered.

Out of the corner of her eye, Sara continued to watch the overturned canoe as it drifted farther and farther away. What if? No, it would not be possible. She was sure one or more of the four shots from the high velocity rifle had hit Allie. Maybe all four.

Within twenty-five minutes, a rescue helicopter from USCG Air Station Clearwater called her on the VHF.

"Sheriff's detective on Calusa Blueway, this is Coast Guard Rescue 6009. We are in your area to commence the search and rescue or recovery. Do you have a flare you can pop to expedite things?"

"Roger, 6009, this is Osprey 4029. Give me five mikes and I will pop a flare above where the canoe is drifting," indicating it would take her five minutes to deploy the flare.

She sprinted around the island to her kayak and got her bug-out bag. She always carried flares in the kayak. Sara sprinted back and shot the flare towards where she had last seen the canoe in the dark. The moon had gone back behind a series of clouds and the night was black.

"4029, Rescue 6009 has your flare. Understand the subject in the water may have sustained gunshot wounds, over?"

"Unknown for sure, Rescue 6009. Probable, but not certain."

Within another twenty-five minutes, she saw the flashing blue lights of a Coast Guard small boat moving her way at fifty miles per hour. Using the heat signature that she and Lynn drew on the Forward Looking Imaging Radar, or FLIR, the helicopter vectored the small boat into her position. A two-man boarding party waded ashore while the coxswain stayed at the helm, idling in the deeper water.

"Y'all okay here?" the female Coastie asked.

"We are. I am Detective Sara Nichols. This is Dr. Lynn Goddard, the County Medical Examiner. Since you guys are armed, please stay here a minute while I go get my kayak and paddle it back around to this side." She handed the now-safe M-4 carbine to Lynn and the Coasties' eyes widened in the dark when he saw the beautiful doctor with the carbine. She looked like a character in a superhero movie.

Sara jogged instead of sprinting this time. As she reached the kayak and bent over to pick up her paddle, something heavy hit her across the shoulders and she went down.

A wet, pained, and tired, but very fit, Allie came down on top of her. Sara rolled and pulled her knees up in a defensive position just in time to catch a numbing blow by a fist to her jaw. Though dizzy and unable to focus, Sara shoved her knees and felt Allie break away from her. Allie rolled to get back on her, but Sara was not there. Sara did a roundhouse swing with her elbow and caught the other woman on the side of the head, taking her down face first in the sand. Sara jumped on her back. Allie reached back over her head, grabbed Sara under both arms and threw her. Sara did an unintended—at least by her—somersault and landed on one shoulder, twisting it. Allie took advantage of the momentary excruciating pain her opponent was feeling and came back, hands around Sara's neck, for the kill.

As Allie tried to squeeze the very life out of Sara, Sara reached under Allie's arms and pushed hard on her chest. Gaining a little working room from that, she rolled back, bringing her long legs up to her chest. She pushed out with her knees, gained more space, pulled her legs up and locked them around Allie's neck. With leg strength borne of years on the beach volleyball sand, Sara squeezed until her muscles hurt. She could feel the other woman's efforts waning and squeezed even harder. She let go quickly, and as Allie fell forward, slid out from underneath and crashed a knife-edge hand chop down on the back of Allie's neck. She was out for the count.

Sara did not have handcuffs, but she took the tactical folding knife clipped to her pocket and cut a length off the line at the front of her kayak. She tied Allie's hands behind her with little concern about cutting off circulation. She picked up the woman and shoved her torso in the cockpit of the kayak, legs splayed out unceremoniously, with feet in the water on either side.

Sara shoved the kayak into the warm water and began to push it around the island to where reinforcements waited unknowingly.

As the male Coast Guardsman saw her coming, he called out to the coxswain twenty feet offshore. The coxswain radioed the rescue helicopter and told it the subject, who he referred to as a "PIW," or person in the water, had been located and was in custody. The pilot advised he was standing down and returning to station. As the county fire/rescue boat came on scene, Sara, now in possession of both radios again, called for it to collect the overturned canoe, now about a quarter of a mile away and take it aboard the boat for transportation back to the office as evidence.

The Sheriff's boat arrived as the Coasties and Lynn were checking Allie for injuries. When they wanted to check the badly bruised face of the detective, she had laughed them off.

Her lieutenant was the first person to wade ashore from the police boat. He surveyed the scene and Sara could tell he was not a happy camper. He tersely asked her how she was. She replied "Sore but relieved this case has come to an end and the suspect would live to be sentenced, then punished for numerous murders."

He turned and walked over to Lynn to check on her. Sara could see the two of them walk away from the

Coasties, paramedics and the prisoner. She watched as they engaged in a lengthy and animated conversation. He walked back to Sara.

"Have you two agreed on your version of this…this… matter?" he asked.

"LT, we have not passed ten words between us since I got here. It was constant action between Allie and me. I was at different places on the island from Lynn most of the time."

"You want to talk now or back at my office?"

"Your pleasure, Boss. I can talk now, if you want."

"You know you broke every damn reasonable procedure by not reporting the abduction of a senior county official and playing one-woman posse, right? You realize you could be anywhere from censured to fired for this?"

"I realize both. There were mitigating circumstances. Had there been a mass alert with a SWAT showdown, I am sure that Lynn would be dead by now, along with the suspect. The only way I could see her coming out of this alive was to play along and unexpectedly take down the suspect. So, I did. Did I break the rules? Yes. Was it the right thing to do? I believe it was the only thing to do, LT. If you want my badge, I will hand it to you right now."

He looked directly at her. Their eyes met in the dark in a long stare. After a full minute, he said, "Subject to the input of the Chief Deputy and the Sheriff, I am going to recommend you keep your badge, but get a damn strong letter of censure in your file. Normally, you might get an award for solving a case like this, Sara. But, under the circumstances, I wouldn't hold my breath for that."

Sara stuck out her hand. He took it in a firm grasp and shook it. The lieutenant then turned and walked back to the police boat without saying another word. Sara let out a breath she had been holding for what seemed to be forever. She was glad it was dark and the darkness masked the tears that followed. She turned, lifted her shirt and wiped them, then walked back to the group on the beach. And, to Lynn.

The fire/rescue team had set up a small spotlight. They were just finishing checking Allie, now in handcuffs instead of Sara's kayak painter. As Sara approached, one of the paramedics motioned her over.

"We need to check you out."

"I'm okay."

"Then why is the whole left side of your shirt covered with blood?"

The crossbow bolt! Mentioning it had reminded her that it hurt like hell.

The paramedics laid her on a disposable blanket and Lynn lifted her shirt. She was wet enough that the blood had not plastered it to her wound. She had a grove in her side, not unlike what a bullet would have done had one grazed her.

"She is going to need some stitches," Lynn began.

"How many?" Sara asked.

"Not many, maybe thirty or so!"

"You are kidding right?"

"Let's let a live-person doctor decide that. My specialty is dead people and you look very much alive."

The paramedics cleaned the wound by flooding it with antiseptic and bound it. They insisted that Sara ride with them in the rescue boat, so Lynn and the lieutenant orchestrated getting her rifle, gear and kayak loaded aboard the police boat for transport back to the launch and retention in the impound lot where the kayak could be protected until she retrieved it. Sara gave Lynn the keys to her Jeep and asked that she drive it to the hospital to pick her up after her multitude of anticipated stitches.

Hour later, with internal stitches and glue that caused the doctor to promise "virtually no scar, just a little white line when you have a suntan," Lynn picked up a still drowsy Sara from the hospital and took her home. Sara went to bed and Lynn fed Gibbs and DiNozzo. She found a tee shirt in one of Sara's drawers and put it on. Sara was sleeping soundly. Lynn crawled in but was unable to sleep. Though she presented a stoic exterior, she was still affected to the very core about having been abducted by a psycho and used as a bait to lure Sara to her intended death. Luckily, her Sara was tough, smart and hard to kill. But, then, so had Allie been.

Lynn laid beside Sara for hours as the detective slept restlessly and the doctor stared at the ceiling. She realized that they were a tough couple. There! She said it: couple. Sara had risked life, limb and career to come get her, just as she had known she would. She would do the same for Sara without hesitation. Finally, she drifted off. She awoke once with a warm spot on her midriff. It was either Gibbs or DiNozzo, she was not sure in the dark. She was not used to sleeping with animals but was finally resting well enough to not change a thing. She closed her eyes as she felt the vibration from his purring. It was strangely relaxing to her, and she was asleep again in minutes.

The next morning, Lynn awoke and it was Sara who was laying there, on her back, staring at the ceiling.

"Hi, Sunshine. Thinking of a new paint color for your ceiling?"

Sara gave her a wry grin and said nothing.

"How do you feel?"

"Is 'like shit' a term used much in medicine?"

"No. We usually grade pain on a scale of one to ten. Using numbers instead of excrement, how do you feel?"

"Somewhere between seven and eight, I think."

"Well, out of the option 'sex, drugs and rock and roll,' I think drugs would be the better answer. They gave you some pain killers at the ER last night. Or, rather, this morning. I will get them and water while you call in sick for a couple of days."

"Can't do that. My career is hanging by a thread. I need to be there in case I need to defend myself. Plus, I have a serial killer to interview."

Sara took her bath in the sink to keep her entire left side dry. She wet her hair in the sink, toweled and blew it dry and put it in a ponytail. Sara knew that a police golf shirt and especially her Kevlar vest would hurt badly, so she put on slacks and a button-up shirt with the shirttail out.

Sara took Lynn to her condo and dropped her off with a very light and careful hug. She was stiff and sore and would be for some time. Only by the grace of God did the bolt not pierce her lung or an organ such as her liver or spleen or kidney.

She parked the Charger and went straight for the lieutenant's office. He was in.

"Morning."

"Morning yourself. How do you feel?"

"Stiff, sore, like I have thirty stitches and a tube of super glue in my right side."

"Do you?"

"I do. Have you heard anything from the Chief Deputy or Sheriff on me?"

"Yep. Got the final judgment right here. They concurred and did this thing fast and conclusively. Read and sign your copy and the one for your personnel file, please."

With some trepidation, Sara took the envelope that Lt. Jaime Gonzalez handed her. It was unsealed and contained two identical letters.

She read them carefully. They were letters of censure signed by Sheriff Rob Roy MacNab. She was strongly censured for not following set procedures and putting herself at grave risk. Nothing was said about putting Lynn at risk. Sara signed both letters, placed one back in the envelope and handed it to the LT.

"I'm not saying, unofficially, that I would not have done the same thing. But, you know we had to do something. This is the least invasive. Case closed. Now, get your butt out of my office and go solve some more crimes!"

Sara said "Aye, aye, sir!" and executed a perfect about face and left. The lieutenant turned away and put his hand over his mouth to hide a smile.

As she sat down at her desk with a groan, Bob, Cindy and Maura came over.

"How bad?" Bob asked.

"A letter of censure. Not as bad as it could have been."

"For whatever it's worth, if I had been the one abducted by a nutcase, I would hope you'd do the same exact thing."

"Thanks, Bob. Don't tell the brass, but I would."

"That goes for Maura and me, too," Cindy said. "We already discussed it and agreed on it."

"In a heartbeat ladies, and I'd want you guys to come for me however you thought would be best, regardless of what's written or taught somewhere."

"You got it. Now. When do you want to talk with Miss Allie?"

"Is she in the lockup or over at the jail?"

"Jail under suicide watch," Cindy responded. "I doubt she would try it, but it gives us an edge in watching her and more security. Plus, she's looney tunes anyway."

"Good move, Cindy! Has she been Mirandized?"

"Saved that for the one who captured her."

"Thanks! We need to establish an address and get a search warrant. There is a reason she has killed so many women and we need to find out what it is. Anything on how she got the canoe?"

Bob spoke, "I just caught a missing person case. A naturalist sort of guy with an old SUV and a nice canoe. The canoe fits the description of the one used to abduct Lynn. And, guess where we found the SUV?"

"Where?"

"The launching ramp at the park where you left from. It was out of sight and the fire boat bumped into it while they were launching it. Had to take the sheriff's boat to another ramp. That's why it was late getting to you."

"Wonder if blocking the ramp was part of the plan?" Sara thought aloud.

"That would fit in with how meticulous she has been with everything else," Maura offered.

Sara said," Maura, would you set up Interview Room 2 and call the jail and have them bring her over?"

"I've done the first and been waiting with eager anticipation for you to say the second!"

"Let's do it gang! Who wants to observe and who wants to partner?"

Bob suggested having one male and one female might be off-putting to Allie, and Sara thought that seemed like a good idea. Cindy agreed and promised that she and Maura would take copious notes, observing unseen. Per recent guidelines, the interviews all had to be recorded with audio and video.

A half hour later, Allie was sitting in Interview Room 2, wearing an orange jumpsuit that did not flatter either her figure or her complexion. She was still stiff and in a lot of pain.

The team let her stew in her juices for a while. Now that she had actually been fingerprinted, they knew who she was. Her military background did not come as a shock to anyone on the investigative team. Generally devoid of tattoos, she did have a small one on the inside of her wrist upon which Sara wanted some elaboration.

Sara and Bob entered the room where the serial killer was shackled.

"Alice May Lang, I am Detective Sara Nichols. We have clearly met before. This is Osprey County Sheriff's Detective Robert Axelrod. We will be interviewing you. You are suspected of having committed a number of murders. Some will be adjudicated here in this circuit, others in their proper jurisdiction. As far as Osprey County goes, probable charges that will be levied against you are as follows. Pardon me for reading, but the list is pretty long: Murder in the first degree of Mary Ann Hixon, Alana Morton, Dolly Woodson, James Remick (he is the canoeist you allegedly carjacked and whose dead body surfaced recently); abduction of Dr. Lynn Goddard; assault on a police officer with intent to kill; grand theft auto; aggravated assault on Leticia Forman, Sam Elston, and Buck Harrison (all at the marina); and, finally use of an explosive device in a terroristic attack. Naples wants you for vehicular homicide, the Florida Highway Patrol for fleeing to elude, Tampa Police for murder of a police officer, murder of a lady whose car you stole, impersonating an officer, and theft of a police vehicle. The Georgia Bureau of Investigation would like to discuss the murder of a Rose Douglas and four other females. I don't believe that I have left anything out. At this time, Detective Axelrod will read you your Constitutional rights per the Miranda Decision."

Bob had set several pieces of paper on the table and began to read verbatim from the top sheet.

"You have the right to remain silent during this or any future interview. Anything you say can and will be held against you in a court of law. You have to right to have an attorney present. Should you desire and attorney and be unable to afford one, the court will appoint one for you at no charge. Do you understand these rights I have just read to you?"

She nodded affirmatively.

"Please answer verbally."

"Yes, I understand."

"Do you waive your rights?"

"No, I do not. I want a lawyer."

"Okay, you need to sign these forms in two places; the first acknowledges that we read your rights to you, the second," and he pointed with his pen," indicates that you wish to have a Public Defender appointed and will only speak upon advice of counsel."

She signed both and Sara unfastened her handcuffs from a steel bar; Bob led her outside, Allie shuffling because of the ankle restraints. He turned her over to the waiting deputy, who took her back to the jail.

"That was anticlimactic," Sara observed.

"You expected any different?" Bob asked.

"No, not really. Now I have to take a ride one county north, unfortunately in a different court circuit, work with the police up there to go to a judge and get a search warrant for her apartment...I suspect the landlord would let us in, but this has to be by the book and I want anything we find to be squeaky clean as evidence."

"Are you good on the address?" Bob asked.

"Yeah. I called the landlord once we got it and the tenant met Allie's description...or, at least her current one, since she changes it to suit the mission. Bob, do you know anything about that female lion head tattoo on the inside of her wrist?"

"No, I don't. Have you searched it on the Internet?"

"No, I have been scrambling just to read her NCIC rap sheet, verify her address from the driver's license and prep for a two-hour interview, in case we had one. Which, unfortunately, we didn't."

"I figured she wasn't going to make it easy for us, Sara. She is one tough, cold ass cookie."

"Yep. Want to go north with me to get a search warrant?"

"Like to, but I have the case on the Remick kid. His autopsy is in a couple hours and I need to be there. We have to put this one away, Sara. She's a one-woman genocide machine."

Cindy and Maura had come into the room as Sara and Bob were talking. The four went the short distance back to their respective cubicles and sat down.

Sara started doing computer searches on the lion's head tattoo, feeling that it might be meaningful to the case.

The closes thing she could find was the Marine Corps Lioness program introduced in Iraq. It put woman Marines in combat units to search for Muslim females who could not be touched by a male, according to Islamic tradition. It had been a success and evolved into a more fully rounded intelligence and security program called FET, or Female Engagement Team.

One of the results of the fingerprint search had been her military service. She had been a Marine and had been given a General Discharge; less than Honorable, more than Dishonorable. Her term of service included Iraq and Afghanistan.

Sara took out her smart phone and scanned names in Contacts until the found the right former associate in NCIS. She called him.

"Hey, Mike. It's Sara Nichols. How have you been?"

"Sara? Damn, I thought you had fallen off the edge of the earth."

"Nope. Hiding right here in paradise. Listen, I have a female serial killer in custody and need some help."

"You all seem to grow those down in Florida don't you. Last one was executed, right?"

"Right. This one may be, too, or she may cop a mental. Her name is Alice May Lang. She was a Marine," Sara paused and gave her duty dates and serial number," and

I want to see if she had special training, like as a FET or something. She got a General Discharge. I'd like to know about why that happened and maybe talk to one of her superiors, if any are still around."

"With the wonder of computers, I should be able to get that to you pretty quickly. That, of course, means Millie and I can stay at your house when we come to Florida for vacation, right?"

"Right! You just provide your beer. Since you are a highly paid federal agent and I no longer am...and, you drink lots of beer once you take your gun is off, it's only fair."

"You always drove a hard bargain, Sara. Done! Back to you as soon as I get this stuff put together."

"Very Special Agent Knowles, you are a jewel beyond compare."

Sara called a friend who was a detective with the De Soto County Sheriff's Office and arranged to meet her to go to a judge up there and request the search warrant. It would have been so much easier, had Allie lived in a different county, but the same circuit.

Forty minutes later, Sara and Detective Sue Dobbs had the search warrant in hand and were en route to Allie's rooming house address. It was in a suburban setting, not good nor bad. They went to the office and the manager escorted them upstairs and unlocked the door after reading the warrant.

"What can you tell us about Ms. Lang? Visitors? Boy-friends? Girlfriends? Drugs?" Sara asked the manager.

"Nothing really. She was Allie Smith to me. Paid on time, always with cash. Quiet. Never a problem. Changed cars a few times in a short period of time, but I figured that was her business."

"No visitors?"

"None that I ever saw."

They went in and the manager went back to the office. The apartment was one big room with a bed, chest of drawers and night stand off to one side, a kitchen against the opposite wall, and a sofa with a coffee table and television in the center. There were several closets and a small bathroom with a tub and shower. Sue looked out the back window.

"There's the parking lot. Totally secure from the street. That's how she could hide the various cars you told me about her 'jacking," she said.

The two detectives already had their nitrile gloves on. The began a thorough search, including the toilet tank, removing every vent cover in the walls and ceiling. Nothing hidden in the usual drug dealer-type places, including the freezer compartment. All in all, the place was tidy, organized with the only thing out of place being the unmade bed. Sara saw blood stains on the sheets. During the entry procedures at the jail, the matrons had said that she was cut up and very stiff and appeared to be in pain. The had the jail nurse check her and had a contracted physician on the way. Sara was aware of the wreck and her going AWOL from the hospital, but she still swam a distance and fought like a demon the previous night. She must have either a high pain tolerance, or the constitution of a cage fighter.

"Hey, Sara. Look at this! Must be her important papers. I have a General Discharge in a folder with a lot of older orders. She was something called a Lioness in Iraq, then a Female Engagement Team member in later Iraq and in Afghanistan. Before that, she was a Marine Military Police Officer, then Investigator at Quantico Marine Base."

"Damn, Sue! No wonder she is tough and knows how to avoid leaving evidence! A military police investigator and then Lioness, then FET. Those ladies were trained like male Marines-pistols, rifles, close combat."

"Sara, it looks like she was, in her last Afghan tour, imbedded in a Force Recon group. Aren't they special operators for the Corps?"

"Yes, though there is a step up called the Raiders. Tier Two. Tough and talented bunch—both. I really need to talk to one of her former superiors now..."

"Okay, Sara, look at this. It's the diary of someone named Rose Douglas."

"That's the name of the first victim, a madam in Georgia. That could give us a hint why she started this rampage—or why the woman's stepson, Allen, did. I still wonder if he was not the killer up there. But, there has to be some connection between them. I will study that one inside and out!"

Sara photographed the apartment thoroughly and boxed the written materials to study as evidence. She and Sue went back down to the manager's office and told him they had left the unit locked and thanked him.

"Sue, I owe you a big one for helping me get the search warrant and doing the search. It makes such a difference if a law enforcement officer who knows the judge accompanies the one from out of circuit to give credence."

"You're welcome! But, I think since your case has gone national, you would have gotten it anyway. That judge is a good one and a good friend to law enforcement. I had a blast coming along and participating in such a biggie, Sara!"

They parted and Sara pointed Argo southward. She had a lot of reading and, hopefully, a conversation with a Marine, to make the case come together.

Several hours later at her desk, Sara had ten pages of handwritten notes to transcribe onto her computer. She had read about how Rose Douglas had taken runaway teen girls destined to prostitution, drugs and maybe death, off the streets and bus stations and put them in her brothel. She wrote that, while they were still prostitutes, they were learning manners, how to dress and take care of themselves and, more importantly, they were out of the danger that the street, pimps, unmanaged johns and drugs would have guaranteed otherwise. Sara, while not an advocate of prostitution, had to agree that Red's way was safer for the girl's than walking the streets. The story bore out what Louisa Love had said, so everything was tying together nicely.

Douglas had worked with her protector and partner, the late sheriff, to move girls to a town seventy-five miles away, and with the sheriff's judge friend in the town, change their names. She had set up each girl, upon her emancipation—when she thought the girl was ready—anywhere from eighteen to twenty-one, in an apartment with the first year's rent covered and a job. The jobs were often at a local manufacturing plant (another friend of the handy sheriff) or as a waitress, with a fast food restaurant...anything but prostitute.

Rose Douglas had carefully listed the girls' original names and their new names and the Social Security numbers she had gotten for them upon emancipation in her diary. The first four names were the Georgia victims. The next names were Mary Ann Hixon, Alana Morton, Leticia Forman and Dolly Woodson.

"Damn! Leticia could have helped by letting me know this. Was she afraid it would destroy her business career? Embarrassed?" Sara silently asked herself.

Throughout the diary, she mentioned her stepson, Allen Douglas, in glowing terms. Interestingly, Sara thought, not sexual or business terms, but like a proud stepmother. Was Louisa Love's take on the relationship colored by her jealousy as Red's lover? Until she caught Allen, she would never know. She still felt that he was a viable suspect for the Georgia murders, but was not sure why. Jealousy on his part, too?

But, the mystery remained about Allie. Why? What was her connection to all of this? She was not listed as one of the emancipated soiled doves. Her age would put her right in the middle of the others, so she had not been too late to list, nor too early. Had she been one of the girls who Rose had not helped for some reason?

Sara was convinced that neither Allie, nor her public defender would admit to anything. She had nothing for which to bargain as a multiple homicide suspect. Sara's other fear was that the rumor already circulating was true; the notoriety of the female serial killer case would attract a national known attorney to defend her *pro bono* for the publicity to his or her firm. And, that as with the infamous O.J. case, the top attorney would slaughter the junior Assistant State Attorney in court. Or, quite frankly, overpower even the State's Attorney, since he may wish to prosecute the case himself to further his political career.

The State's Attorney had set a meeting in his office at 5:00 PM, and that was less than an hour off.

The case was of such prominence that he was to run the meeting, and his assistants, the lieutenant, chief deputy and likely the sheriff would be in attendance. Sara, and since the canoeist's body had just been recovered floating, Bob, whose case that was, would be the primary presenters. This would be a prosecutorial strategy session.

Bob had to scramble for his presentation; the body had only a slit throat as corroborating evidence. He had asked Lynn to put off the autopsy scheduled during the rush meeting so that he could attend the legal session instead.

The two detectives and lieutenant walked over to the State Attorney's Office in the courthouse together. The chief deputy and Rob Roy MacNab arrived moments later. They met in a large conference room, with the senior prosecutor at the head of the table. Pads and bottled water were sitting at each position.

State's Attorney Smythe opened, as was expected.

"We all know each other and have worked a myriad of cases together over the years. But none will have the national, maybe international, coverage of this one. I have had confirmation that Ms. Lang has fired her public defender and that a nationally recognized defense attorney has taken her place." He mentioned that attorney's name, and his fame and perhaps notoriety was such that no further discussion of his stature was required of the group assembled around the table.

"I have already contacted my counterparts in Naples, Tampa and in Georgia. We have first shot at Ms. Lang. Nobody but Tampa's circuit seems to have a tight homicide case, unless we have more evidence than I currently know. Naples has a good vehicular homicide, but that's not enough for this woman. Sara, give us an executive summary of your case to date."

Sara took the next thirty minutes describing the crimes, the case and her findings. The prosecutor summarized.

"Then, Sara, we have a good case on battery on two at the marina, the bomb thing against Ms. Forman, two incidents of attacks with intent to kill against you, a police officer, and three murders with no physical evidence, except for *modus operandi*?"

"Almost, Mr. Smythe. On the Dolly Woodson murder, the last one, we have witnesses who I believe with a picture array, will place her in the area of the murder at the proper time, so as a non-attorney, it is my opinion that adds "corroborative" to "circumstantial.""

The prosecutor nodded and was deep in thought. After several minutes, he asked. "Sara, have you determined how she was able to pull this off and, maybe the big one: why?"

"Yessir to the 'how.' She was a Marine Corps MPI, or military police investigator. She left that to join the

"Lionesses" in Iraq and later, their successor the Female Engagement Teams, or FETs. That helps to explain her ability to not leave evidence, her attack skill set and her toughness to kill a police officer while seriously wounded and to do a long swim in order to put up a darn good fight against me only days later. She's smart and tough."

"And, clearly crazy," the Sheriff MacNab observed.

"I think so. I am waiting to speak with one or more of her Marine Corps supervisors to get a read on her. Indications so far suggests to me that she suffers from PTSD and that her final lack of discipline in a war zone earned her the General Discharge. But, that is a verbal interim report from a friend at NCIS. I hope to have more in the next couple of days."

"Bob, tell me about your victim," the State's Attorney asked.

"He was late twenties and kind of an environmental hippie who moved from one river guide job to another. The only valuable thing he seems to have had to his name was the nice canoe that Lang stole before she allegedly killed him."

"No autopsy yet?" the senior prosecutor asked.

"No sir. We just fished him out an hour or two ago. The only thing we know is that he had his throat slit. We got his junker SUV out of deep water at the launch ramp where they left from earlier and the forensic team has not found any evidence that could be used in a murder investigation."

"We can charge her with his homicide and wish for the best, based on M.O., location and her possession of the dead boy's canoe. I am not convinced we will win a conviction on that, based on our adversary at the defense table. Neither am I convinced that we have enough evidence to feel confident about the Hixon, Morton and maybe Woodson murders either. Georgia has virtually no evidence on the five there. Tampa may have the best murder case, along with

Naples's vehicular homicide. If she gets consecutive instead of concurrent on all of these, she will be put away for life. Or, she may get lethal injection on killing the police officer, probably not on the lady in the Mercedes. No witnesses, just the gun she stole," he summarized.

"We will fight like hell in the court room, but, I am afraid that in perhaps ten instances, Alice May Lang will have gotten away with murder. That is no reflection on the investigative work done in four jurisdictions, it's just the way it is."

After a few dejected moments, the attendees rose and without conversation returned to their offices to contemplate, re-read material and hope for an unanticipated admission.

CHAPTER 13

Sara received a text from a Marine Major Andre Close. He offered to talk with her via Skype from Afghanistan and was available currently. She acknowledged and they set up the call on her smart phone.

"Major, thanks for reaching out to me."

"My pleasure. I understand you used to be an NCIS agent, what caused you to go local?"

"Ha! Too many trips to places like you are calling from! I just got tired of traveling three hundred days a year. Tell me, Major, how did you know Alice May Lang?"

"I knew her first time around when I was a first lieutenant. She was a Lioness and a damned good one. Her military police experience made her a good searcher. That's primarily what the Lionesses did. They searched Muslim women that a man was unable to touch due to religion and custom. She went on to be a FET. Do you know what that is?"

"Yessir. I do."

"Before I go any further, detective, why are we having this conversation? What did she do?"

"She will be charged with eleven murders. They are spread through Georgia and Florida."

"Holy shit!"

"My sentiments exactly. And, she was so adept at killing and not leaving evidence, she will likely skate on most of them."

"Wow! Detective, she was really good at what she did. I bumped into her again as a FET on my second tour in Afghanistan. She was starting to have troubles then. She clearly had PTSD and we actually spoke unofficially. I liked her. She was a good Marine. She had, over time, as a kid who spent her life in orphanages and foster homes, grown to hate her birth mother. It seemed to have become a burning obsession with her."

"Major, do you know what her birth mother's name is, or was?"

"No. I don't think even Corporal Lang did at first. But, I think she found out around ten years ago on a trip home to the US. That was under my watch. She came back different. I got orders to report to Marine Corps headquarters and we parted. When we met again a few years ago, she was different. Really different. She was having trouble obeying orders. Her interactions with the Muslim women as well as her own Marine compadres were becoming strained. She was being very violent with the women and that's what caused the General Discharge in lieu of court martial."

"Interesting. You said she found her mother's name out around ten years ago on a trip back to the States?"

"Yes. She came back different, as I said. Hard to explain. Kind of like her attitude went south. Wind went out of her sails. She did her job, but instead of enthusiastically like before, she seemed to plod along at it."

"Did the Corps consider PTSD treatment instead of the discharge?"

"The incident that caused her discharge was serious and I am sure is still classified. She was lucky, PTSD or not, that she got kicked out instead of going to Leavenworth.

I guess in view of what you have told me, Leavenworth might have saved a bunch of lives?"

"Maybe some in Florida, Major. I think she had already killed in Georgia on her furlough. I just have to find out who her mother was. I think I have the answer in a diary that I have not finished reading. Does the name Rose Douglas ring any sort of bell?"

"No. Afraid not."

"Major, you have been a great help. There is a remote possibility that I may need you to rehash this in a notarized signed, sworn statement. Would you be willing to do that?"

"I would. Of course, I'd have to have someone from Navy JAG with me."

"Of course. Thanks for your service over there. Be safe."

"You, too, detective."

Sara immediately went back to the diary and read it until nine at night in her cubicle. Nothing about Red Douglas being the mother of Alice May Lang. She called George Abernathy, the retired GBI agent.

"Hi, George. It's Sara Nichols from Florida. Sorry to be calling you so late, but I have the serial killer in custody."

"Good show! How'd you get her?"

"She was caught, in the hospital in Tampa, killed a Tampa police officer and a society matron, kidnapped our county medical examiner, shot me with a cross-bow, and I ultimately beat the crap out of her."

"You are a piece of business, Sara Nichols. Thank Jesus you are on our side!"

"Yeah. I'd make an awful crook. But, you may have the answer that will explain this whole case. What was Rose Douglas' maiden name?"

The retired agent paused for a minute thinking. Then he uttered one word.

"Lang."

"That is what I was hoping you would say. She was the suspect's birth mother, who gave her up for adoption at birth. I have a diary of hers that names every victim, including one who has managed to stay alive. They were all hookers with Rose, who Rose protected, got their names changed, gave a grubstake to and went on to lead, however shortly, honest lives. The one who has avoided Rose's or Allie's razor has even been highly successful, thanks to the good-hearted madam."

"Since you have her, you will be trying her in Florida. Hang on to that diary. We will be needing it up here in Georgia!"

"Will do! Please advise the GBI agent working the case now about what I told you. I will be glad to talk with him at any time. All I need to find out now is what happened to Allen Douglas and if he was involved in any of these murders—particularly his stepmother's like Louisa Love seems to think. He left, according to Louisa, about the time of Rose's murder.

"And, George? Anything you can do on the Georgia end to come up with birth records on Alice May Lang, anything that ties her to Rose as her daughter would be great. I will work on it here, but y'all probably have the best and quickest shot.

"You have really done some work on this. I will talk to my successor and have him call you. Glad that crazy woman is behind bars. When the case is over, come up and we will go after Gentleman Bob. I have a Fox double in sixteen gauge that is only a hundred years old, but you will love it anyway!"

"You are on! Even if I don't kill anything myself, I will enjoy watching you and that pointer work. And, I will help you and your wife eat the quail breasts."

"See you soon then."

Sara made a note to herself to get with Maura tomorrow and really dig for the birth information. If she, in fact, killed her mother and the girls that Rose had given a better start to than herself, the reason was pay back for being abandoned and jealousy for the other girls and their better shot at life…gratis, Rose Douglas. And, that would be the "why" that had been so elusive.

Sara called Lynn and chatted briefly, advising her that she was heading home after a long day.

Once home, she fed the cats and took a hot bath. Sara put on a thin, almost transparent tee and sat on the bed, cross-legged, her laptop in its namesake place.

She felt, more than saw, the two cats tense. Looking up, she saw a tall, blondish man aiming what appeared to be her pistol at her.

"Allen Douglas, I presume? Look just like the artist's rendition of you."

"Detective Nichols. I am going to call you Sara, though our friendship will be a short one."

"You have to tell me: why did you kill those women in Georgia?"

"I only killed one woman in Georgia. That despicable piece of garbage stepmother of mine who made me have sex with her at fourteen and made me available to disgusting men at her loathsome whore house."

"Then, who killed the four women in Georgia?"

"Your captive, Allie Lang. Abandoned daughter of Rose Lang Douglas. I put an end to my stepmother's miserable life and left. Allie showed up immediately, stole the razor and the cash and got a list of the girls Rose had helped—the one halfway decent thing my father's second wife ever did."

"How did you escape being a suspect?"

"I had a good alibi the exact time she died. Fake, but solid. Then, I moved in with my uncle, the sheriff, and he taught me how to be a man-tracker. So, I was with him each time the other girls were killed. And, since they were my friends and one was the only person, other than my uncle, who I ever loved, I decided to use my skills as a beginning, then later, a damn good bounty hunter, to track down and kill the daughter. But now, my perfect crime of getting away with the murder of my piece of shit stepmother is at risk. Because of you. Allie is a psycho. She may blurt out that she killed the four, but that she found Red freshly dead when she got there. And, I will be under suspicion. But, only you know the parts of the story that can tie together and hang me. So, you are going to commit suicide."

"I think your reasoning is a bit flawed, Allen. More people than I know the story. You kill me and you will just add death of a police officer to death of a madam a decade ago to what you will have to answer for."

"I have made up my mind. And, you have made it easy. I am going to shoot you with your gun at a suicide distance, wipe the gun and put it in your hands, and type a suicide note on the computer in your lap. Then, wipe the keyboard and put your dead fingerprints all over it."

"I don't particularly want to die, tonight. I think we should discuss the logic of your plan a bit more. I can help you."

"No!" He raised Sara's 9mm Sig with two hands.

"Crack! Crack! Crack!"

Allen stood there and looked Sara in the face. Then, he fell forward onto his own face. Dead.

Dr. Lynn Goddard, wearing a damp bath towel, stood ten feet behind where the tall man had been. She lowered her snub-nosed .38 and let out a long breath. She switched into medical doctor mode and walked over to the body. Switching the revolver to her left hand she touched two fingers against his carotid. He was dead. Dead as hell.

Sara, brave as she was, sat there on the bed shaking. The two looked at each other. Sara got up, pulled on a sweat suit over the thin tee shirt and dialed the direct number for dispatch.

******

Detective Cindy Leton took the ME's statement. It was corroborated by the statement that the LT took from Sara. It was a clean shoot. Tomorrow, Sara would call the GBI, once Allen Douglas' admission had been put in transcript form and advise them that the murder of Rose Douglas a decade ago had been solved, and there was no trial to have to worry about. Most of the loose ends were tied up. Allie may well get the lethal injection for murder of the Tampa police officer. She would get varying sentences for most of the rest. Vehicular homicide was a lock-in. The terroristic assault with an IED against Leticia Forman had a living victim and lots of witnesses. The prosecutor felt that sufficient circumstantial evidence existed on the last murder...Dolly Woodson...that he could get a conviction on that. As to the rest, she would have gotten away with murder. Just as Allen Douglas almost did. Several weekends later, Sara and Lynn joined Leticia on her Mako fishing boat for an all-girl crew for a fishing tournament. Another member of the crew was Sally, who seemed to have developed a close relationship with Leticia. They did not win the tournament, but caught dinner and laughed for four hours, something Sara needed to do in the midst of the Osprey trial against Allie Lang.

It took three months, but Allie was found guilty of the assaults and plea-bargained the murder of Dolly Woodson down to manslaughter. She had the best justice money could buy and was found not guilty for the homicides of Mary Ann Hixon, Alana Morton and the canoeist. But, Sara suspected that the evidence in the Naples vehicular homicide and Tampa policeman's murder was too over-whelming even for Allie's Hollywood lawyer. Justice would be done and she would never walk free again.

******

Later, during Florida's second season, when it went from hot to not-quite-as-hot, Sara and Lynn drove to Miami. They had an ambitious itinerary laid out.

First, a weeklong cruise of the Caribbean on a luxury liner. As promised, the detective paid. Following that, several days fishing and visiting with Sara's professional fishing guide brother and his family in the Keys and two days and nights at Fantasy Fest in Key West.

They would stop at a spa in Naples for full treatment on the way back to Osprey County, where they would resume their lives…and their next adventure.

THE END

If You Liked This, You Might Like:
City On Fire by Dallas Barnes

FORMER HOMICIDE DETECTIVE, DALLAS
BARNES, PROVIDES UNNERVING SUSPENSE AND
SHOCKING INSIGHT ON CHILLING SEX AND PREJ-
UDICED CRIMES.

Detective Sergeant Lee Hollister is an experienced cop
who is finding justice is an elusive goal as it snakes its way
through contemporary society. He silently hopes his life
choices aren't a reflection of what he sees wrong in others.

Detective Bobbi Marshal is an attractive woman
whose beauty turns heads. Ironically, she and her partner
comprise the LAPD Wilshire Division sex team. Bobbi,
mature, sophisticated, capable and compassionate, finds
herself working and competing in a man's world.

Detective Sergeant Stryker and Detective West are a
"Salt & Pepper" team, one white, one Black. Besides race,
there's one crucial difference between the men…at End
of Watch, Stryker drives out of the ghetto into a White
community where he lives. West has a much shorter drive,
his home is in the ghetto.

Now, it's just a matter of time and cunning …and who
makes the first fatal mistake.

**City on Fire includes: City of Passion, Badge of Honor,
Deadly Justice, See the Woman and Yesterday Is Dead.**

AVAILABLE NOW

About the Author

G. Wayne Tilman is a full-time author. He retired from the Federal Bureau of Investigation several years ago. Prior to the FBI, he was a Marine, bank security director, deputy sheriff, investigator, and security contractor.

He holds baccalaureate and master's degrees from the University of Richmond and has been an adjunct faculty member there, as well as the University of Phoenix, St. Petersburg College and Florida Metropolitan University.

Some of his law enforcement subject matter expertise includes threat assessment, continuity of operations, security and executive protection, counter intelligence, international terrorism, and small arms. He has been an instructor in those subjects in a number of training academies, conferences and seminars. Mr. Tilman holds the internationally-recognized Certified Protection Professional board certification, generally accepted as the highest in the security profession. He also earned a US Coast Guard 50 Ton Inspected Vessel Master Captain's license.

G. Wayne Tilman's primary interests are family and writing. His avocations are bushcraft (survival/primitive camping), hiking, boating, kayaking, shooting sports, and travel.

He wrote his first novel over thirty years ago and has now written thirteen novels. Genres include espionage thrillers, mysteries, and Westerns.

G. Wayne Tilman's impetus to write in those genres comes from both personal experience and heritage.

A direct ancestor was a sheriff in Virginia Colony in 1680. Another ancestor was the lawman who brought in outlaw Bill Doolin singlehandedly and helped to decimate the infamous Doolin-Dalton outlaw gang, sometimes known as the Oklahombres. Bill Doolin was the Desperado of song fame. Closer to home, his mother was a counterintelligence agent for what is now the Defense Intelligence Agency or DIA.